AISHA

A Tale of Retribution

"Merely to come into the world the heir of a fortune is not to be born, but to be still-born rather."

Henry David Thoreau

"AISHA"

"Hi there, Sir Rowling," Daniel Madden slumped into one of the comfortable chairs of the airline's first class lounge. The man he had addressed, sitting directly in front of him, was Christopher Rowling, a British diplomat and an old acquaintance. Rowling scoffed and fidgeted without looking up from his newspaper. He had recognized the voice, of course; the American journalist's tone irritated him, but then again, all Americans did. After a calculated moment, he finally looked up over his reading glasses towards Daniel.

"I' m not "Sir" yet, so don't jump the bloody gun, now will you, Madden?" Rowling had the habit of calling people by their family name only; it was his very British way of establishing superiority over them. Daniel Madden, like any pureblooded American, couldn't have cared less. For him, it was a level of useless subtlety, or hot air, wasted hot air, that is. He had gotten used to British sarcasm and their obsessive need for the double *entendre* in just about everything they said, regardless of the listener's ability or not to comprehend the double meaning. He loved this little game that the British played, for him it made them predictable and in a way, easy to deal with. Rowling returned to reading his copy of *Le*

Monde Diplomatic, or at least he was trying to do so, and therefore diplomatically ignore Madden's presence.

"Oh, but you're on your way to London for that big ceremony now, Christopher, everybody knows that. It's no big secret, you know." The other's stiffness and tight upper lip amused Daniel. He had learned to know Christopher Rowling very well over the past seventeen years. As chief correspondent for a major American newspaper covering the Middle East, it was impossible not to know him; he was, after all, the most senior British diplomat in that region, and had been posted just about everywhere, from Iran to Egypt, as well as many countries of the Persian Gulf. Rowling was a respected and highly appreciated authority on the region. He knew everyone, was very well connected, and as such, journalists like Daniel often solicited his opinion, mostly off the record of course. Their paths had crossed many times over the years; in a region dominated by wars, oil, opulence, misery, medieval royalty, and Islamic extremists, there was always something going on for a journalist or a diplomat. Both knew the region extensively and were familiar with its players and numerous crises. They had an ongoing love-hate relationship, as British and Americans sometimes do. Rowling looked up from his paper again.

"I certainly hope you are aware of my knighthood. It was all over the bloody news. You're a journalist, aren't you? Really, Madden, sometimes you astound me. All I was saying was that I'm not 'Sir' yet, so don't address me in that way. It's bloody bad luck."

"Oh come on, Christopher. I was pulling your leg. I was joking, ok?"

"I certainly hope so, Madden. Well…" Rowling looked around the lounge with a resigned look. "I guess there is a bright side to being stuck in this airport for any amount of time. I mean, seeing as I am apparently also stuck with you, that is. At least it won't be too much intellectual exercise, if you see what I mean now, Madden?"

Daniel ignored the barb; it only meant that Rowling was warming up to his presence.

"Now, don't be mean, Christopher. What do you say we have a drink? That should cheer you up. Oh, come on, they said the delay could be as much as six hours."

Rowling sighed, and put his newspaper and glasses on the table beside him.

"We might as well, I guess. Bloody Frenchmen, you can always count on them to mess things up. What is this air traffic controllers' strike anyway? It should be illegal. I mean, how long are we supposed to be stranded in this godforsaken place?"

"Hey Christopher, let's make the best of it, ok? I mean, look on the bright side of things. We are in a comfortable first class lounge and we have all this time to chat about our favorite subjects, right?" Daniel stretched his arm in the direction of the door, amused at the other's discomfort. For Daniel, this first class ticket was a treat, a treat that his boss at the paper would never have authorized, the cheap bastard. No, this little treat had been the doing of Natalie, his on again off again girlfriend of the past seven years. Natalie's job at the airline had permitted this little upgrade, which Daniel appreciated greatly, considering the situation.

"Very well then, Madden." Rowling let out a huge sigh. "Let's go then, what the hell, but I warn you, the first round's on you."

"It will be my pleasure, Christopher. As a matter of fact, I am feeling generous today and am willing to foot the whole bar bill, no problem. Now how's that for generosity?"

Rowling did not answer as they headed towards the bar.

The bar was full and animated, as all flights were delayed. Rowling and Madden found a perch at the end of the bar.

"Gin and tonic please, and a whiskey on the rocks for my friend here," Rowling pointed to Daniel, who acquiesced with a nod. "Good memory, Christopher. Make mine a double will you please," Daniel added.

"So Madden, where are you off to? You seem to be heading in the wrong direction, away from the action."

"Yeah, tell me about it. I have to go back stateside at least four times a year, you know, for meetings and such. It's one of those trips, a long, boring week at the office." Daniel, like all foreign correspondents, was addicted to the "action," as Rowling had put it, the constant traveling to new countries and cities, the hunt for the story, and of course the proximity of others who did the same job as he, colleagues and friends, who had become his family over the years. He missed them already.

The two hung out at the bar for a few hours, sharing stories about the war and its effect on regional politics. After a number of drinks, Rowling loosened up a bit and the conversation became lively and animated. As seasoned professionals, they respected each other and everything else set aside, they actually had a liking for each other, although neither one would have admitted to that.

They had been at the bar for just over three hours when an announcement was made. All flights were cancelled due to the strike and would be rescheduled the next day.

"Blasted French, they do upset me so." Rowling had turned red and was obviously very displeased at the turn of events. Like all diplomats, he did not like anything that was unexpected. Madden, on the contrary, couldn't have cared less. Some extra down time at the expense of the airline, booze and food included; he had no qualms with the program.

"Hey Christopher, they'll be putting us up in a good hotel and they'll be paying for it. The situation isn't that bad now, is it?"

"No, I suppose not, but I am expected in London, you know. I bloody well hate this."

"Well, your knighthood ceremony is set for next week, so what's the rush? You'll get there on time, don't worry."

"Very funny, Madden, hilarious I might add, come along now; let's go catch that shuttle to the hotel, bloody French," Rowling was seething. Of course, the fact that the trains did not work either was the drop that really ticked him off. In a gesture of pure French solidarity, the railway unions had decided to support their colleagues, the air traffic controllers. The only way out of Paris was by bus or by car, both possibilities that were uninteresting because the roads would be jammed up.

On the shuttle ride into Paris, Madden decided he'd try to change Rowling's disposition.

"You want to have dinner later, Christopher? I know a great restaurant in the *huitieme*. Fantastic cuisine, great wine, I'll tell you what; I'm inviting you, ok? Let's say it's to celebrate your knighthood. Is it a deal? I mean, what else is there to do? You gonna sulk in your room all by yourself? What do you say, "Christopher?"

"Well, you have a point there, Madden. What else is there to do? I suppose there is no harm in accepting your offer, since I am officially retired from the service and it could not be perceived as patronage. Therefore, I accept, and I will add that it is mighty generous of you, Madden, and I do appreciate it, thank you." Rowling's mood had shifted slightly for the better.

"Think nothing of it, Christopher. It is my pleasure, so shall we say around eight? I'll take care of the reservation when we get to the hotel."

"Eight is fine, Madden. Let's meet in the lobby at seven-thirty, what do you say?"

"Seven-thirty is fine. Good, now you're talking," Daniel smiled to his companion, who smiled back, although it was only half a smile, restrained, as it must. After all, forty years of diplomatic reserve could not be erased that easily. There were certain habits that were encrusted in Rowling's brain.

The dinner was most enjoyable. The food was excellent, accompanied by the finest wine. Their host, Jean Pierre, had exquisite taste and was well educated. He knew exactly how to treat a grumpy conservative English gentleman like Rowling. He even succeeded to make him laugh a few times, which was no small feat. Rowling was having a howl of a time, as he put it. His face was flushed from the wine and he actually had a real smile hung upon his face. They were halfway through their second bottle of *Cote Rotie*, when he looked at Madden with a wry expression on his face.

"You know what, Madden? I might, I just might, I say," Rowling stressed the word might, "have an extraordinary story for you." Madden became alert; the word story had sobered him up instantly.

"Considering this excellent meal which you offer me and for which I repeat, I am very grateful to you, I am willing to reveal the intimacies of this story, but at certain very strict conditions." Madden was about to speak, but Rowling signaled to him to be silent.

"Now this story, my friend, is most explosive and any association of my name as the source or possible source would be catastrophic to the British Foreign Service and to my memory as a faithful servant of said service. Needless to say, should this get out with my name attached to it, I would not be Sir Anything. Do I make myself perfectly clear, Madden? You must swear that you will never, under any circumstances, drag me into this."

Daniel put his hand on his heart. "I swear, Christopher, that whatever you say will eternally remain between us. I swear on my mother's grave, Christopher." Rowling had piqued him and Daniel wanted to know more. Career diplomats like Christopher Rowling who said they had a story, now that had to be more than worth the listen.

"Very well then, you most certainly have heard of Prince Abdul Khalid Mohamed Al-Turki and his mysterious and untimely end?" Madden became all ears.

The excesses and lifestyle of Prince Al-Turki were common knowledge to anyone familiar with the region, womanizer, heir to the throne, and royal pain in the ass for a very concerned and media-shy royal family. Many unflattering stories circulated on his subject, yet no foreign journalist had ever been able to interview him or even less, had an inside view of his private life or palace. A palace, which was guarded day and night by a small army of guards it was said, guards whose loyalty was fierce and deadly for any trespasser who would have dared to try to enter without permission. Madden listened intently; a story about Al-Turki and his life and death was sure to be good. The journalist in his blood began to boil. Without waiting for a response, Rowling continued.

"Well, in the last seven years of my service, I was, as you know, attached to the British Embassy in the kingdom of his father. Officially, my job was senior commercial attaché. It was a job that I did not occupy for long, however. Being an accomplished bridge player, I was often invited to the ambassador's residence for a game. The King himself was often at the table and during the course of our evenings playing bridge, we became quite friendly; a most civilized chap, I might add. Anyway, one evening during a break, he pulled me aside and asked me if I would be so kind as to pick up the game with his son the Prince, who had an excessive attachment to the game but few qualified partners to play with.

" I told his highness that I would be more than happy to oblige him, but that of course, I would have to check with the ambassador first. The ambassador graciously accepted the

13

King's request. So in the name of good diplomatic relations, I was sent off to play bridge with the Prince in his palace. Because you see, Madden, that was the inherent condition, the games were played at his palace, nowhere else. The Prince was a most unusual person, I must say, especially when it came to bridge. I don't think I have ever met someone so taken with the game, yet so incompetent. Anyway, with two other partners, palace employees, we played sometimes for ten to fourteen hours nonstop. The Prince was obsessed; of course, the alcohol he drank did not always help, but I was not there to judge, I had a job to do, that's all.

"After a few months of this, the ambassador asked me to devote as much time as necessary to the Prince. The King had expressed his satisfaction as to my services, so it practically became my full-time job to be the Prince's bridge partner. For the last five years of my service, that was my principal function. Of course, I became very intimate and close, and was considered a permanent fixture of palace life. The rhythm of our playing was irregular. Sometimes we would play four or five days in a row and sometimes we went a week without playing. It was during one of those bouts of excessive play that I noticed her for the first time, a strikingly beautiful girl of about eighteen or so, a beauty so uncommon, that it practically knocked the breath out of me. She was rather on the tall side, five feet ten or eleven, I would say. Her hair was silky black and fell below her waist. Her eyes were dark and intense and she had the finest sculptured facial features. She walked and moved slowly, always upright and there was a musicality in her movements and one could feel her strength and perceive that she was inhabited by a richness of spirit and profoundness of soul. All this I sensed without having spoken a word to her. She was more than a beauty, you see, Madden; she was an angel of sorts. I mean, forgive me the expression, but I know no other way to express the stunning effect this person had on her immediate surroundings. It was something that I had never perceived or felt before, in all my years of wanderings with the Service. I stress this point, but do not get me wrong about my intentions here, Madden," Rowling became defensive. "My loyalty to Gertrude over the past forty-four years has been unflinching and steady. I was not attracted to this girl, she fascinated me. Anyway, it happened occasionally that she served us tea during our games. The Prince was always very harsh with her and he would constantly abuse her verbally. At the same time, he could not get his eyes off her when she was not looking; her mere presence made him most agitated. He was obviously very taken by this girl. She, on the other hand, never reacted to his verbal abuses in our presence; she went about her business, distant and proud.

"One day the Prince asked me if I would accept to be her teacher. He told me that she was a highly intelligent girl that had learned Arabic in three months and that she had this crazy fascination with America and wanted to learn more about it and to perfect her English. After checking with the ambassador, I accepted and so two times a week I began to give this girl lessons. Her name was Aisha Sayuno, and the story I promised is about her. Still interested, Madden?"

"Christopher, I am riveted to your every word."

"Very well then Madden, there is a condition to you knowing the whole story."

"Ok, and what may that be?" The expression "whole story," had pricked his ear.

Rowling leaned over and retrieved a small briefcase from under the table. He opened it and pulled out a thick, black hardcover notebook.

"Now, this notebook contains a manuscript which was given to me by this girl a few weeks before I left the region. It is the story of her life, told by her in the most exact and troubling details. I give you this manuscript to read, then at

your best convenience, I will fill in all the blanks for you."
He handed the notebook to Daniel.

Daniel began to say something, but Rowling put a finger to his mouth. "Hush now, Madden, you read first and then the questions, do we agree?"

"We agree, Christopher, I must say that I'm most anxious to read this, you've whetted my appetite to the extreme, a story about the Prince, now that smells like a scoop to me."

"Just remember, Madden, absolute, total secrecy. I have your word as a gentleman, don't I?"

"Absolutely Christopher, you have my solemn word."

"Very well then, what do you say we have ourselves a little Armagnac?"

"Agreed, *garcon,*" Daniel motioned to the waiter.

They finished their drinks and were soon on the way back to the hotel.

Inside his room, Daniel took off his shoes, poured himself a drink, sat down and opened the large notebook that Christopher had just confided to him. Once he began to read, he could not stop; so taken he was, by the incredible story that burned up every page. He read well into the night, taking notes as he went. The next morning, a very agitated and sleep-deprived Madden crisscrossed the lobby in search of Rowling. Finally he caught up with him at the concierge's desk.

"Can you believe this, Madden? We are stuck here until this evening. These incompetent Frenchman can't bloody get us out of here before."

Daniel ignored the statement, as did the concierge, as only the French can ignore something that is said which they understand perfectly but pretend not to.

"Christopher, may I speak to you now? It's rather important."

Rowling looked at the agitated and disheveled Madden. "What's gotten into you, Madden? You look like you haven't slept all night"

"I haven't, Christopher, so please bear with me, will you?"

"Ok, let's go sit over there." He pointed to some large chairs in the hotel lobby.

For the next few hours, Daniel peppered Rowling with questions, jotting down answers hastily. He wanted to know every detail that surrounded the story of Aisha Sayuno. Rowling obliged him graciously, providing all the information he needed to understand the "whole story," as he had said on the previous evening. Madden was excited as hell.

"Come on now, Madden, calm down. You look like you'll have a bloody heart attack over this. Get some sleep now, will you, forget about it for a few hours. If I would have known it would set you off like this, I would have been more cautious."

Daniel did not reply; he got up. "Thank you, Christopher. Please excuse me; I have to go to my room now."

"What the hell for, Madden?" Rowling looked up at him, a surprised look on his face.

"To write, Christopher," he shouted over his shoulder as he briskly headed for the elevators.

A perplexed Rowling shouted to him as he jumped into an elevator. "Keep me posted, will you?" Madden waved his hand to him in a gesture of affirmative reply.

"Bloody Americans, what a strange bunch," Rowling said out loud to no one in particular, as he rose and headed for the newspaper shop, still fuming from, "Madden's most impolite and abrupt brush off."

Daniel put the do not disturb sign on the door and sat at his computer. For the first time in a long time, he was inhabited by a powerful and uncontrollable urge to write.

Words and sentences gushed out of him like the cold, clear water that pours powerfully from a pregnant mountain stream in the springtime. He was in a trance, oblivious to his surroundings or physical state; he was inhabited by "his" story. For four days and nights, he stayed in his hotel room and wrote. He ordered food from room service, refused to let them clean the room, and did not answer the phone, which rang incessantly. Obviously his very furious editor wanting to know what in the hell he was up to. On the third day, Daniel ripped the phone line out of the wall. He would let nothing prevent him from immediately recording for posterity the incredible story of Aisha Sayuno. The world had to know about this, he intended to make sure of that. On the fourth night of his seclusion, he finished the story. Meticulously he reread his work. *The Story of Aisha Sayuno by Daniel Madden.*

Aisha Sayuno was born in the Philippines, Manila to be exact. Some of the poorest people on earth live there, and Aisha was one of them. Here, misery was the *plat du jour*; it was omnipresent and reigned supreme. The poorest of the poor were so accustomed to their miserable state that they considered "her," almost as another person. For yes, in this part of the world, misery is feminine, real misery that is.

Aisha and her family were among the most unfortunate of the earth. Her father pushed carts at the docks for a living. It was hard physical work, fourteen or sixteen hours a day, just to make enough money to feed Aisha, her mother, and four younger sisters. They lived in a shantytown on the outskirts of Manila. There was no running water, no electricity, houses were made of bits of wood, cardboard, and metal found here and there. All was patched together in an unbelievable array of small and disheveled abodes, each more decrepit than the other. Streets were dirty, narrow, and infested with all the byproducts of its inhabitants' paltry existence. From this scorching quagmire of devastated humanity rose a stench so powerful that a strong wind could carry it many miles away. Mixing in with the stench was a cacophonic din of voices, shouts, tools banging, and dogs barking, the all, becoming, a surreal crescendo in the symphony of despair. The inhabitants of the shantytown were so used to the noise, they didn't hear it anymore, but to a visitor or unaccustomed observer, the din was overbearing and most disturbing.

Here, if you were sick, you died; if you were weak, you were trodden; if you became old and useless, you were discarded and forgotten. It was a place that had only one rule; survival, survival by any means possible. The family unit was all that offered protection and security against a heartless and unforgiving world, a world, which offered no light, no warmth and worst of all, no hope. No hope whatsoever, for the abandoned and dehumanized souls who were the unwilling byproducts of countless corrupt governments and the mercenaries of savage mercantilism. It was in these surroundings that Aisha Sayuno was born.

From a very young age, it was apparent that Aisha was different; she was not like the others, she was highly intelligent, sensitive, mature, and always willing to help the old, the poor, or the sick. Soothing them with her words and touching them gently with her hands. All loved her; she was a beacon of light. Her humility and purity of spirit were equaled only by her immense beauty and strength. No task for her was too demeaning, no human being unworthy of comfort. Aisha was an inspiration to all, especially to her mother, who was very proud of her.

Aisha had only one luxury in life, and that was school. A congregation of nuns ran a school on the outskirts of the shantytown and there, she devoured knowledge like others do food; she was insatiable. She wanted to know all there was to know about the world and the people in it. Although she was very passionate about school, her family obligations came first however, helping her mother cook, clean, wash, and take care of her little sisters was number one.

Her mother had a part-time job in a factory two days a week, and on those days, Aisha stayed home and took care of the children. The factory was far, on the other side of the city and her mother had to leave at five-thirty A.M. on the days she worked. It was a large factory owned by a foreign company that employed many people. They made clothes there that were sent to America and Europe. Aisha's mother spent twelve hours a day at a sewing machine and was back at eight at night totally exhausted. It only paid her a few dollars a day, but they needed the money desperately.

Her father would stumble home at night well after the children were asleep. In the light of their gas lamp, he would eat the rice and beans his wife had prepared for him. She would always wait for him to eat, even if she had had a long, tiring day at the factory herself. They would whisper in the light of the lamp, so as not to wake the children. Aisha was not always asleep, and she often heard him ask, "And so, how are my five Princesses?" Although he knew that all these girls were a burden, he loved his wife and all his daughters deeply. He would have given his life for them. Those quiet moments, in the semi-darkness, by the light of the lamp, were all the intimacy her parents had. The one-room dirt floor hovel they all lived in, did not allow for anything else.

Aisha felt a lot of pain for her parents who worked so very hard, for so very little. One day, she promised herself, she would leave this place and become someone in the world and she would return to help her parents and her sisters. "They will live and eat well and never be in want again, I'll see to that," she solemnly swore to herself before going to sleep at night. It was not a prayer or a wish she made; it was a threat, a threat to the forces of evil that had condemned her and her family to their miserable existence.

Then, one day, when Aisha was thirteen and a half, tragedy struck. As often in the life of the miserable, when they believe that the worst is already upon them, then something even more terrible hits them. Such was the fate of Aisha, her mother and sisters on that dark and unforgettable September evening.

Aisha had been back from school for a while and was helping her mother prepare the meal for the children, when Mr. Cantor came running up to their humble abode. Mr. Cantor was Aisha's father's supervisor at the docks. He ran into the house, sat down, and while he was still trying to catch his breath, he half-shouted and half-wailed, "Oh, Mrs. Sayuno, a great disaster... has happened. I'm so sorry, a large container overturned, it was an accident, such a terrible accident. I'm so sorry; he was killed instantly. I'm so very sorry." He was looking at Aisha's mother with a mixture of sorrow and confusion.

Aisha's mother just stood there in shock and disbelief. She put a hand to her stomach, as if she had been struck there. Her body began to tremble and she dropped the pan she was holding, and it fell with a thud to the earthen floor.

"My Faisal is dead, is that what you are saying, Mr. Cantor? This cannot be true. No, no, no, tell me this is not true, Mr. Cantor, please, tell me this is not true." She fell to the floor on her knees, and crawled to where Mr. Cantor was seated and grabbed him by the knees.

"Tell me this is not true, Mr. Cantor, please." Her voice was high-pitched and she became hysterical, wailing and crying uncontrollably, her whole body shaking out of control. Mr. Cantor put his trembling hand on her head,

"I'm afraid it's true, Mrs. Sayuno, I'm so sorry. I do wish I had better news, but I don't."

His last words were buried by Aisha's mother's uncontrollable screaming on the floor at his feet. Mr. Cantor looked about the room, not knowing what to do, or how to comfort this poor, broken and devastated woman at his feet. Neighbors began arriving at the door, to see what all the commotion was about. Two of Aisha's mother's friends came inside and kneeled beside her, trying to comfort the devastated Lina Sayuno. But, it was to no avail, the pain in her entrails was too extreme. Aisha's four younger sisters stood near the sleeping part of the room, holding unto each other in the semidarkness, crying and unable to understand the full force of the tragedy that had just struck them; only aware that something very wrong had happened. They did not realize that their sole provider and protector was gone and that they were alone now, five young girls and one woman, poor and vulnerable against an unforgiving world.

Aisha walked across the room and helped her mother's friends lift her mother from the floor. She took her mother's frail and shaking body into her arms.

"Oh Mama, Mama, what will we do?" Tears rolled down Aisha's cheeks.

"I don't know my child, I don't know." She hung onto Aisha desperately.

Aisha kissed her mother's cheeks and said through her tears,

"I am here Mama, I am with you, and I will help you." She held her mother's tortured face delicately in her hands, her eyes fierce and brave as only the young can be when confronted with insurmountable odds. Lina Sayuno remained inconsolable

Faisal Sayuno was buried the next day; a few neighbors, Mr. Cantor, and some men who had worked with him, all came to briefly acknowledge the passing of Faisal Sayuno into the other world. Quickly they left, to go back to the urgent matter of survival. All they left his devastated wife and five daughters were words; words of love, words of hope, words of sympathy, but still only words. In a world, which had no time or patience for the weak and the disadvantaged, Lina Sayuno and her five young daughters were in the worst of situations.

After her husband's death, Lina Sayuno received help from the neighbors and the nuns. Of course, she knew this was only temporary, as no one had much to share. After a week, she ran out of money.

"Aisha, my love, I must go to the factory to try to get more work, five or six days a week I hope. I will be back later. Please take care of your sisters?"

"Yes Mama, do not worry, I will take care of the house and the girls."

Aisha knew from that moment on that she would have to quit school. Her mother would work and she would take care of the children and cook and clean. It broke her heart, but she knew that there was no other way and that's just how it would be. She wished she could go to work, but at thirteen and a half, she was too young. Plus, her sisters were eleven, nine, five and three and they needed her now, they needed her more than ever.

Her mother came back that night after dark, tired from the walk and hungry. Aisha served her some rice she had kept hot for her.

"They will give me four more days' work. I start tomorrow; you will have to quit school you know."

"I know, Mama, but do not worry about that. I will take care of the children and the house. Later, I will go work too," she said confidently, although her heart was broken.

"I wish you could have finished school. I wanted so much for you to get ahead in the world." With those words, Lina Sayuno began to sob silently and Aisha put her arms around her.

"Its ok, Mama, everything will be all right. I will help you, I promise. Together we will make it, you'll see."

Lina Sayuno looked at her daughter and smiled, "Thank you, my love, thank you for those comforting words. I love you, you know."

"Me too, Mama, I love you too."

They ate their meager meal of beans and rice in silence, their faces shining listlessly in the light of the lamp; each lost in her thoughts and enveloped in the folds of their common desperation.

The next morning at five A.M., Lina Sayuno raised her small, sleep-deprived body; she quickly ate the leftover rice from the night before, and left in the darkness on foot for the factory. It would take her an hour and a half to get there. She carried with her a little bag, which contained some rice and beans for her thirty-minute lunch break. The work at the factory was long, boring work, but it would feed her family, and that's all that mattered to her. The factory employed over 800 workers, all women, and most worked part time as Lina had done before. Lina loved the feel of the pants and blouses that she sewed; they were so soft and so pretty. She wondered about the people who would wear them and how they lived. "They must be very rich to afford these," she concluded. But mostly Lina worried about her situation, her meager salary and how to make ends meet. She knew she would have to earn more money, because what she would earn at the factory would not be enough, even with the extra days she would be working. The nuns had been helping her a bit, but they could not do that for much longer, she knew she would have to find a solution and soon.

Her most pressing problem however was the distance to the factory, to walk three hours every day to and from work took everything out of her. She was so tired that sometimes for a second or two; she would fall asleep at the sewing machine. This frightened Lina because she could lose her job. She heard from other workers that some of them had set up under a highway underpass near the factory. It was far from the ideal place, but it was out of the rain and only a ten-minute walk to the factory. It could be a solution to her most urgent problem. Rhea, one of her friends who worked at the factory, had offered to Lina to show her the place. She had been living there with her family for a number of years.

"I think we could make room for you and the girls," she had said. "I have talked to my husband. We will all help you build a shelter. It is not that bad, Lina, you'll see."

So, Lina Sayuno moved her family and her scant possessions from the shantytown that had been her home forever and into a hovel made of cardboard and wood under an underpass, there was no running water, no power, and the ever present odor and noise from the highway above. Rhea, her husband and sons were of great help and very kind. The shelter they built was rough, but Aisha made it cozy and warm. They all slept on mats on the cardboard-covered floor and the cooking was done on a small gas burner. Water was fetched from the river below and was boiled, for it was brownish and smelled. Aisha did all the cooking, cleaning, and laundry. She took care of the children, making sure that they did not stray on the highway, singing to them, and telling them stories when they were sad. She kept them clean and warm and was extraordinary at a most difficult time in her family's life. Her mother adored her.

"What would I do without you?" she would say. "I really don't know."

"It's ok, Mama, please don't worry. I'm fine, the children are fine, so don't worry, please," Aisha would plead with her every night. She was becoming very concerned about her mother's health and saw that she was getting weaker and suffering greatly from the strain of their situation.

It was at about that time that a co-worker spoke to Lina about a man who had helped many desperate people like her. His name was Mr. Chen and he represented a group of very religious and wealthy people who helped people in need. The co-worker had a friend whom he had helped in the past and she told Lina that she would see if she could arrange a meeting with him for her. To a desperate Lina Sayuno, it was the answer to all her prayers and sounded almost too good to be true that such a person should exist.

Two weeks later, she met Mr. Chen after work, in a little park, not far from the factory. He was a short, stocky man, a mix of Oriental and European and was about forty. He was elegantly dressed in a beige suit with a matching hat. A distinct scent of fine cologne emanated from him and his hands were impeccably manicured. Never had a man of this demeanor spoken to Lina Sayuno before, she waited in silence for him to speak.

"Good evening, Mrs. Sayuno, I suppose," he extended his hand in her direction, "I am so sorry about your husband, life must be very hard for you."

"Yes, indeed Mr. Chen, life is most difficult." Lina took his hand limply, she was uncomfortable, he was obviously an educated and influential man, and she was not used to speaking with people of his rank.

Feeling her discomfort, Mr. Chen smiled warmly and pointed with his extended arm to a bench nearby under a large tree.

"Come, Mrs. Sayuno, let us go sit over there."

They sat on the bench, facing each other. Delicately, Mr. Chen crossed his finely manicured hands and cleared his throat.

"Mrs. Sayuno, I have a proposition to make you, which I am sure you will find most interesting, considering your situation." The fact that he called her Mrs. Sayuno intimidated Lina even more and she stared to the ground at her feet.

"You see, I am an agent for some very select and very rich clients, clients who live in other countries and who are prosperous and powerful people. Some, some are Princes and some, yes, some are Kings." He widened his eyes and got closer when he said the word Kings, so as to emphasize his point. "Now in the goodness of their hearts and because they are very religious people, they have asked me to scout the world to find exceptional children living in poverty or in difficult situations. The idea is to find a way to help these children in their education and advancement. To help them get ahead in the world and make their life better." On and on the elegant Mr. Chen went with his marvelous story of faraway benefactors and their goodness and their desire to help the unfortunate. Although his words were music to Lina's ears, she wondered if it was all a dream and if such places and people really existed.

"Only the chosen few are sent away, Mrs. Sayuno, to a far-off country to complete their education. They are under constant supervision of the highest quality, in the most comfortable of surroundings and in a very strict religious environment. Finally, but not the least important, there is money in this for the families of those who are chosen, sufficient money to pay for those things which would otherwise be impossible to buy." Mr. Chen paused; he let the last sentence sink in. It had caught Lina Sayuno's attention. Although Lina was still not sure where he was going with all this, she did not dare interrupt him.

"So, Mrs. Sayuno, to get to the point, your daughter Aisha has been brought to my attention. I understand that she is an unusually brilliant child."

The mention of her daughter's name sent a little shock wave through Lina's heart.

"But Mr. Chen, she is only thirteen and a half, a child still, and I need her so much to help me with the other children while I work." Lina was alarmed.

"Oh, but I understand and I have thought of this, Mrs. Sayuno," he smiled warmly, trying to be reassuring. "If we make an arrangement concerning your daughter, she would stay with you for four more years and at seventeen and a half, she would leave for her educational trip. After five years, she would return here and do as she pleases. She will have been educated, fed, taken care of, and she would even have some money of her own." He continued quickly, the word money had had its' desired effect on Lina Sayuno.

"Speaking of money, if we make an arrangement, I would give you one hundred U.S. dollars a month for the next four years and two thousand dollars as a lump sum the day she leaves for her educational trip. Now that is my offer Mrs. Sayuno."

Lina was excited; this was the money she so desperately needed. She could buy enough food at last and clothes and medicine for the children. She remained cautious however and hoped that her excitement did not show too much.

"Of course," Mr. Chen continued, "All this is conditional to me seeing your daughter, speaking with her, and making sure that she is a good choice."

Lina eyes flickered, she had to think quickly and she knew she could not let this opportunity pass her by, even if she had apprehensions.

"I understand Mr. Chen, but tell me, will she be able to write to me? Five years is a long time to be away." Lina asked the question more to stall and to have time to think than to actually get an answer.

"But of course Mrs. Sayuno, she can write as often as she wants. That goes without saying and also I will give you news of her on a regular basis."

It was all too much for the vulnerable and uneducated Lina Sayuno. She took a deep breath and said, "Mr. Chen, your offer is very kind and very generous. It is a great honor to have thought of my daughter. I would like to think this over and talk to my daughter. Do you think we could meet again, tomorrow or the day after, if that is more convenient?"

"Please, Mrs. Sayuno, take your time, there is no hurry. Tomorrow will be fine. I will be here at the same time. Believe me, I understand that this is a lot to consider and I am at your service in this matter." Mr. Chen rose and tipped his hat in her direction, "I bid you good night now and will see you tomorrow." With these words and without waiting for a reply, he was off into the night.

Lina whispered good night as she stared straight ahead, lost in her thoughts and troubled by what she had just heard. She sat a long time on the bench, thinking about her conversation with him. The money he proposed was the answer to all her prayers, but she was worried about her Aisha. Aisha her precious love, her everything. Would she be safe? Could she trust this Mr. Chen? When she got home, these troubling unanswered questions were still spinning in her head and she went to bed very unsettled that night.

The next morning when she rose, her mind was made up. She would say yes to Mr. Chen, yes for her family, yes for her Aisha. Anyway, four years gave her all the time she needed to check him out and to see if he paid the money. Time was of essence to her decision. Tonight she would meet Mr. Chen and accept his offer and then speak to Aisha about the importance of his upcoming visit.

That night when she came home after her meeting she told Aisha of her encounter with Mr. Chen and how educated and well dressed, and wonderful he was. How he had heard about their predicament and Aisha's brilliance, and that he had chosen her to help her. She also explained about the money and how critical it was to their situation. "In four years, you will get the chance to get out of here and into the world, my love. It is a unique chance that will certainly not come again."

Aisha was thrilled and scared at the same time. "But Mama, I will miss you all so much. I don't know if I can leave you."

"Yes you will, and you can, my child. You will do it for us and for you. In the meantime, it will allow us all to live better. You understand, my love?"

"Yes Mama, I understand and I will meet Mr. Chen on Sunday. I will be my best, I promise."

"Good girl, you will see, he is a very nice man who only wants to do good for his very generous and religious clients." They hugged a long time in silence and then went off to bed. For the first time since her husband died, Lina Sayuno slept soundly.

That Sunday, Aisha and her mother met Mr. Chen at the bench under the tree as Lina had not wanted him to see their dire abode. The meeting went well, Mr. Chen was charming and Aisha was shy and did not say much. Her mother helped the conversation along. After an hour or so, Mr. Chen said, "I must go now, Mrs. Sayuno. Thank you for coming Aisha, it was very nice meeting you." Aisha blushed and lowered her eyes. "I will be back here on Wednesday at the same time Mrs. Sayuno, so as to conclude our affairs. Good day to both of you now."

That Wednesday, Lina got her first hundred dollars from Mr. Chen. She clutched it tightly and nothing or no one could have dislodged it from her hand. Mr. Chen got up, tipped his hat, and said, "I will see you next month Mrs. Sayuno, same time, same place; good evening to you now."

Lina reached out and took his impeccably manicured hand and kissed it. "Thank you, Mr. Chen, thank you, you have saved our lives. God will remember you, you are a good man."

"Think nothing of it, Mrs. Sayuno; it is my job, I am happy to be of service." With those words, he turned and walked away. Had it not been so dark, Lina might have seen the wicked smirk on his face. "He had done it again," he thought to himself. He was content at his performance, content and amazed at the naiveté of people. "People in need will believe anything," he concluded, "if the conditions are right, of course." With that thought in mind, he disappeared into the night, chuckling to himself.

The next four years flew by. The children grew up, Lina worked hard, and Aisha took care of their humble abode without ever complaining about her lot. They had enough money to feed and clothe themselves. Life was not great, but it was bearable. Aisha's sister Kyle was now fifteen and taking over a lot of the household chores in preparation for Aisha's impending departure. Aisha and her mother never talked about her departure, but on her seventeenth birthday, her mother said, "You know you will be leaving soon, my love. I will miss you so much, you know."

"So will I, Mama. I will miss you all terribly."

"Happy birthday, my tender love and never forget I love you more that anything in this world." Lina took Aisha in her arms and held unto her tightly.

"So do I, Mama, so do I, I love you." They held each other thus for a long time, each shedding some tears in silence and sadness.

Mr. Chen had kept his side of the bargain; the money had always been there. Sometimes Lina would not see him for many months. It was another man who brought the money, a man who worked for Mr. Chen. He was a silent somber man who never said a word and would just give her the money and leave. In four years, Mr. Chen had never missed a payment, but Lina was worried. There was a secret side to Mr. Chen that she now knew about, a very secret and a very terrible side that she did not dare tell her daughter about and it devoured her night and day. Everything had gone fine for about a year and then, one night that she had gone to pick up the money, Mr. Chen had asked her to sit down on the bench beside him and he had told her his life story and how lonely he was, traveling all the time and how his wife had died a few years before and that he had never remarried. Lina had listened politely and when he was finished he had taken her hand and had placed it on his private parts. Lina had been in shock, but she had let him have his way, for she could not live without his money.

So every month when he was around, Mr. Chen would abuse her; in the worst way a man can abuse a woman. Lina suffered in silence for her family, there behind the tree, close to that bench, in the dark. She felt like vomiting every time, but she dared not, for fear of insulting him. When he was done, he would zip his pants, tip his hat, and without a word, would be off. Lina would stay there every time, shaking, crying, upset, and sick to her stomach. This was the man who would soon be leaving with her Aisha. That very thought terrified and tormented her. It haunted her night and day. Yet, there was no going back; it was too late, the deal was done. She dared not think what Mr. Chen might do if she tried to get out of the arrangement. In a short while, her Aisha would be off, but to where? What would happen to her? She shuddered when she thought of what might await her poor little girl, so she prayed in those last six months. She prayed a lot and she hoped that God, for once would be on her side.

The last time she saw Mr. Chen on the bench, she fell to her knees and begged him to promise her that nothing would happen to her daughter. Weeping, she grabbed his leg and pleaded, "Please Mr. Chen, I will do anything you want, I will be yours forever to do as you wish, just do not harm my poor child, please."

"But of course, Mrs. Sayuno, all will be fine. Believe me, you are alarmed for nothing. Now come sit with me, get up from the ground now, woman. All will be as I told you; you are concerned for nothing." He went on to tell her all he had said already, trying to be as reassuring as possible. Lina Sayuno was not convinced, but she kept silent.

Then the day came. It was a dark day for Lina Sayuno and her heart was filled with anguish. She wept and clutched her daughter on the bench, near the tree where she had been so often abused by the very man Aisha was leaving with.

"Write to me my love, write to me every day; promise me you will?" she managed to say through her tears.

"I promise Mama, I promise I will." She was crying too, unable to fully understand her mother's devastation. For a long time, she looked back at her weeping mother on the bench as Mr. Chen led her away.

Not a word was said between them as they walked for about ten minutes and reached a road where a large dark car was waiting for them. Mr. Chen opened the door for her. A driver sat up front. Aisha was amazed at the softness of the seats and the coolness of the air. Soon they were off, speeding along a highway.

They arrived at an airport hangar where a large private jet was parked, door open, steps extended. The car drove straight up to the plane. Mr. Chen stepped out, and helped Aisha out of the car and onto the plane. Aisha was impressed by the interior of the plane, but then again she had never been on a plane before, or even near one. The seats, the curtains, everything was from another world, a world that she had heard about, but had only imagined. Now she was in this world; she was excited and anxious to see the rest.

There were two other men on the plane. They wore dark business suits and were sitting at the back of the plane. They both had thick mustaches and dark sunglasses. They rose to meet Mr. Chen and shook his hand and bowed their heads slightly in his direction. They spoke a language which Aisha could not understand. She would learn later that it was Arabic. The men went back to their seats without having acknowledged her presence verbally or by eye contact.

Mr. Chen went to the front of the plane and spoke to the pilots. Then he came back and buckled Aisha's seat belt. A steward closed the door and the plane began to move away from the hangar. Soon they were moving very fast on the runway and then, they were airborne. Aisha had butterflies in her stomach, it was the most incredible sensation she had ever felt in her life. She was amazed at the feeling of being in the air, like a large silent bird. She gazed outside at the fast-moving landscape in total awe.

They flew for a very long time. They slept and ate a few times; the steward was very efficient and polite. Mr. Chen asked Aisha every few hours, "Are you ok? Do you need anything?"

"I am fine, Mr. Chen, thank you very much. Tell me, when do we arrive?"

"Soon, child, do not worry, then you will see how lucky you are to have been chosen." He smiled his warmest smile and Aisha smiled back. At that precise moment in time, she was the happiest she had ever been in her life.

Mr. Chen looked at her as she stared out the jet window. At seventeen and a half, Aisha had grown into an incredibly beautiful young woman. Her thick black hair fell to her waist and swayed sensuously with every movement of her head. Her features were refined—slightly pronounced cheeks, a long delicate forehead, slightly curved lips, but mostly it was her eyes that were striking. They had fire and brilliance, tenderness and strength, sensuality and defiance. They were the mirrors of her purity and immense beauty. Her body also had grown. She was tall for her age, with long elegant limbs, that were in perfect coordination with the blossoming of her physique. Aisha was a rare beauty; she was the marriage of the best of human physical and spiritual elements.

"In a year or so," Chen thought, "She will be the finest of the fine, the prize, the crown jewel. Oh Prince Al-Turki will be happy about this one; his royal blood will most certainly boil. Plus, so cheap, well, cheap for me, but expensive for him, as it should be," he concluded, chuckling under his breath.

They were flying over desert now. The sun was rising, magnificently brilliant in the distance; the plane began its' descent and the steward picked things up. The two men in the back spoke rapidly amongst themselves; they seemed excited. Mr. Chen buckled up and Aisha did the same, by herself this time; she was a fast learner.

Soon they were on the ground. When Aisha walked out of the plane, she was blinded by the sunlight and astounded by the heat. "So hot," she thought, "yet so early in the day." A large white car was parked close to the plane. It was very long and had at least six doors. Aisha was impressed; it was the first time she had seen a limo. Two men sat up front. They were in black suits like the other two on the plane. Aisha sat in the back with Mr. Chen and the two men from the plane sat facing them. No one spoke and there was an awkward silence. Aisha stared out the window. The landscape was empty, only sand as far as the eye could see and the occasional hut or house in the distance. After a ten-minute ride or so, the car arrived at a gate, a massive iron gate with guards in army uniforms in front of it. They wore a white cloth on their heads, which was held down by a red headband. Aisha had never seen such accoutrements on soldiers. They saluted the car as it passed through the open gates.

They sped down a driveway that was lined with palm trees and multicolored flowers and bushes. It was very beautiful and in sharp contrast with the barren and desolate landscape they had just seen. In the distance, Aisha could see buildings, eight or nine of them. One was much larger than all the others. It stuck out because it was so large, but mostly because of its' dome. The dome was immense and was covered in gold paint, or so she thought at the time. The light of the sun hitting it created the impression of a beacon, as a lighthouse beacon, powerful, blinding and visible from a great distance. Unbeknownst to Aisha at that time was the fact that the dome was in fact covered in eighteen-karat gold. It had been built at the request of Prince Al-Turki, so as to convey to his visitors his immense power and unfathomable wealth. Everywhere that Aisha looked, there were guards, gardeners, or people at work.

The car pulled up to a building just off from the main building. Six men dressed in white robes came running out. They were all young, obviously in fine physical shape, and had their heads shaved. They formed a line on each side of the car doors, staring to the ground. Immediately behind them appeared another man, older, a tall and strong man, who by his movements was obviously in charge. He wore the same robe as the others, but it was of a very bright red with rich gold trimmings about it. His hair was cut in a brush cut and he adorned a large thick mustache, which curled at the corners of his mouth. On the left side of his face was a long, ugly scar, which caused one of his eyes to droop slightly and it gave a sinister aura to his already imposing person. His name was Mohamed Al-Zahrani, ruler supreme of the "House of the Pure," house which lodged the numerous women of Prince Abdul Khalid Mohamed Al-Turki.

The Prince, first in line to the throne, horseman extraordinaire, hunter and charmer, had a volatile and fiery temper, equaled only by his unimaginable wealth. It had been said that the Prince had once plunged a dagger through an immigrant servant's heart, killing the man instantly, all because the tea the poor man had just served him was cold. Such a man did not confide the supervision of his woman to just anybody. Mohamed Al-Zahrani or Mr. Za, as everyone called him, was a cruel and ruthless man and was well known for his brutal and violent behavior towards anyone who dared defy him. He spoke few words, made no mistakes, and was totally loyal to his master, the Prince. It was well known that he personally executed any man under his supervision that broke the rules of the House of the Pure.

The rules were simple; do not stare, do not speak and do not touch, under any circumstances, the Prince's women. Mr. Za himself had selected all inner palace guards, in the orphanages of the poorest countries of the world. He bought the young men from crooked administrators when they were between four and eight and he would then send them off to his training camp, where they were castrated and put through a very intense and grueling training that lasted years. Mr. Za personally supervised the training of his guards until they were eighteen or twenty and ready to take up their service at the palace. Their loyalty was absolute and total to Mr. Za; they obeyed his every command instantly, without questions or hesitation. All of them had been raised, knowing that to break a rule or to disobey an order meant certain and immediate death.

The door of the car opened, Mr. Chen, Aisha, and the two men who had been on the plane stepped out, all shook Mr. Za's hand and bowed slightly. They spoke in Arabic, so Aisha did not understand what was said. The two men in suits got back into the car. Mr. Chen turned to Aisha. "I will be going now. I leave you in the excellent care of Mr. Za. He will take charge of you. Do as he says, be polite and obedient, and all will go well. I will be back from time to time to see how you are doing."

Aisha turned to face Mr. Za. He and the guards intimidated her; it was all so strange and exciting. She turned to say goodbye to Mr. Chen, but he was already in the car and it was moving away. Mr. Za stepped sideways and motioned with his hand the direction to go. In a soft, kind voice he said, "Please follow me, Miss, it is this way."

Without another word, he led the group up the stairs of the House of the Pure. Aisha followed his huge body and the guards walked on either side of her. They were tall, silent, strong, and intense. Aisha felt minuscule in their midst and was very impressed to be part of such a strange procession.

They walked down endless corridors, covered with thick, colorful carpet. Everything was out of proportion, on a grand scale. The height of the ceilings and the doors, the ostentatious chandeliers, even the vases, tables, and chairs, everything was large or excessively ornate, and reeked of limitless riches. Occasionally they passed by some maids at work, who all wore a pretty light blue uniform with a delicate white fringe. They would stop work when the group passed them and bow their heads, staring to the floor.

Finally, at the end of what seemed an endless corridor, they came up to a large double door with two guards in white standing before it. They bowed their heads and opened both doors to let them by. They went down another long corridor, except this one was all in shades of pastel pinks and blues. At the far end, Aisha could see that there was a pool and people, but it was too far for her to distinguish anything clearly. On each side of the corridor, there were doors every thirty feet or so. Some doors were open and Aisha saw some girls in them. She locked eyes with one of them for a fleeting second, as she passed by with her entourage. She was a young woman, a year or two older than Aisha. Her hair was blonde, and her large blue eyes seemed so sad to Aisha. She was very richly dressed and was sitting on the edge of a bed. She smiled to Aisha as she passed; Aisha timidly smiled back.

Mr. Za stopped in front of one of the doors. He opened it and walked in. Aisha followed him in. The six guards stayed outside. Aisha loved the room instantly, the huge bed, the thick rug, the bathroom with its large bath, the soap, the towels, everything. For a person of such humble origins, it was mind-boggling and beyond anything she had ever imagined.

"Now, my child," Mr. Za spoke in a low and very soft tone with a slight and unusual accent. "You must be very tired from your trip. I suggest that you take a bath and sleep a few hours. There are new clothes in the drawers and wardrobes." Mr. Za opened the drawers and wardrobes to emphasize his point. "I will be back in six hours to give you some information about how things work and show you around. When you awake, if you wish to eat or drink something, just pick up the phone over there and order what you want. Is all this clear?"

"Yes, sir, very clear, thank you sir. It has been a very long day and a few hours' sleep will be welcome. Thank you very much, sir, for everything." Aisha was too tired or ashamed to tell him that she had never used a phone before in her life.

"You are welcome. Please call me Mr. Za; it is how I am called around here. So, if there is nothing else, I will see you in a little while."

"No sir, Mr. Za, there is nothing else."

"Good, then be sure to be well-rested by tomorrow, for tomorrow you will meet the master." Mr. Za's eyes widened when he said the word *master,* so as to stress the importance of that encounter.

With those words, Mr. Za turned and left the room, leaving Aisha standing there, minuscule in her ocean of splendor, in total awe and unable to move for a very long time.

After a while, Aisha slowly walked towards the bed. She passed her hand on it, to make sure it was real. She touched everything else; all was so soft, so new. She stepped out the open double doors onto a small, flowered balcony, looking at the magnificent grounds and vegetation. Tears rolled down her cheeks. "I am in heaven," she thought, "oh how I wish Mama was here to see this."

It took awhile for her to figure out how the large, modern bath worked, but eventually she got it. For the first time in her life, she took a long, warm bath. It was divine and incomparable to washing in the dirty river back home. She then crawled into the large double bed and got between the sheets. It was the most exquisite sensation she had ever experienced. She slept for five or six hours. When she awoke she was hungry and disoriented. It took her ten or twenty seconds to figure out where she was. She picked up the phone and put it to her ear, as she had seen a nun do once at the small office in the school. Immediately a voice came on the other end.

"Yes Miss, how may I help you?" The voice was female, and the person spoke with the funniest of accents.

"I'm hungry," was all she could manage to say.

"I will bring you something Miss, in about twenty minutes." The person did not wait for a reply, but hung up. Aisha was left holding the receiver for a moment. Slowly she put it back in its cradle. She made her way outside to the balcony, and sat down in one of the comfortably cushioned chairs that were shaded by a large white parasol. She felt calm and serene, in harmony with the beauty and the silence of the moment.

A short while later, someone knocked on the door. Aisha got up. A woman bearing a tray walked in. The woman was short and thin, of about Aisha's mother's age and physical appearance. Her hair was tied down tight and she had a round, painted dot in the middle of her forehead.

"Hello Miss, how are you today?" The woman put the tray down on the table under the parasol.

Pointing to the tray, she said, "I brought you some orange juice, some fruit, cereals, and some sandwiches. So come eat now." She took Aisha's arm and led her gently to sit back down.

"Thank you, you are so kind."

"Hush now, child, it is my job. I am here to take care of you. My name is Mohini. When you need me, you pick up the phone like you just did."

"Thank you. My name is Aisha, Aisha Sayuno."

"I'm pleased to meet you Aisha, now go on, eat."

"Thank you Mohini," Aisha smiled.

Mohini smiled back. "You're welcome. I'll see you later then, child." Mohini left. Aisha would later learn that Mohini was from India, which explained the funny accent and the painted dot on the forehead.

Aisha began to ponder on the last thing that Mr. Za had said to her, "tomorrow you will meet the master." There had been something ominous in his voice when he had said that; it made her anxious and a little nervous. It sounded so important. As it turned out, it was not only important, it was everything.

The next evening, Aisha met for the first time, his Royal Highness, Prince Abdul Khalid Mohamed Al-Turki, unbeknownst to her at the time, was the fact that the Prince was a man who spent his mountains of money on every extravagance imaginable, especially women, young women that is. His palace, at any given time, housed between twenty-five and forty "guests" as they were called, to the great dismay and disappointment of the royal family. The royal family tolerated the Prince's excesses, so long as he was discreet and contained his lifestyle to his palace. The Prince obliged them with joy. At thirty-two, he was in his prime; he was a tall, strong, and elegant man, who carried himself like the royalty he bore. His complexion was dark, as were his eyes, which were full of the fire and fury of an Arabian stallion. He was always impeccably groomed and his long fine fingers, which were manicured daily, could either caress or kill. The Prince, it was well known, could be as lethal as he was charming; he was not a man to be put to the test. Of course, Aisha ignored all this at the time. She was still swimming in her adolescent illusions of being there for her education, sponsored by very religious and rich benefactors, as Mr. Chen had told her and her mother.

Mr. Za came to fetch Aisha. She had been sitting in a chair when he knocked. She rose when he entered; she was excited and had butterflies in her stomach. Aisha had done as he had said and worn some of the fine clothes that had been put in her room. She had washed her hair, which fell loose and shiny to her waist and wore no makeup, for she never had and did not know how to apply it. Makeup or not, at seventeen and a half, Aisha was an astounding young woman and a sight to behold.

"Mr. Chen has been right about this one," thought Mr. Za. "For so many years, he has been promising the Prince a rare and unique beauty. He will be complimented by the Prince for this one, a fine choice," concluded Mr. Za as he eyed Aisha with his drooping eye.

"Are you ready, Miss?"

"Yes Mr. Za, I am ready."

"Tell me, girl, what is your name, so that I may introduce you properly to the Prince?"

"Aisha, Mr. Za, Aisha Sayuno."

"Very well Aisha Sayuno, now, you will also be meeting some of the other guests of the Prince tonight. Just remember to be polite, not to speak out of turn, and that we all owe the Prince the utmost respect and attention, as he is our host and protector. Is that clear to you?" His tone was serious and laden with authority.

"Yes, Mr. Za, it is perfectly clear." Aisha couldn't wait to meet the Prince, she was anxious to express to him, her and her family's profound gratitude for having brought her to his palace and taken her under his wing.

They walked down the long, lush corridors. The white-clad guards were everywhere, at every door and window. Aisha noticed for the first time that when they passed, the guards would stare to the floor. They reached two very large high doors that two guards opened for them. They stepped into an immense room, which had a high dome-shaped ceiling. The room was lit with candles and lanterns, the odor of incense filled the air, and exotic Arabian music played in the background. A heart-shaped podium was central to the room. Scattered loosely around the podium in groups of twos or threes were girls, all kinds of girls, maybe thirty or forty in all. At each extremity of the room, food and beverages had been laid out on low tables placed on richly colored carpets. The girls were sitting or standing in small groups, eating, drinking, and chatting amongst themselves. They all stopped talking when Aisha walked in with Mr. Za. Everyone turned and looked at her and she was very intimidated by their stares. Mr. Za walked through the girls and up the three stairs of the podium. He clapped his hands and said, "Ladies, may I have your attention, please?" The girls gathered around Mr. Za and listened. "Allow me to introduce to you Miss Aisha Sayuno," he pointed in Aisha's direction, "a new guest of the Prince. Please be kind to her and help her become comfortable. Thank you for your attention, now carry on. The Prince will be here shortly." Mr. Za left the podium and went off to one side. One of the girls approached Aisha, the one she had briefly seen as she had passed in the corridor on the day of her arrival.

"Hi, my name is Alina, Alina Kabayeva." She extended her hand and Aisha timidly took it.

"Aisha Sayuno pleased to meet you."

"Come, I will introduce you to some of the other girls."

"Thank you," Aisha smiled and followed her shyly around. Alina escorted her and introduced her to everyone. Aisha was polite, smiled, and said hello to all. The girls were from a variety of countries, Pakistan, India, Indonesia, Thailand, Sri Lanka, Turkey, Russia, and so on. There were four other girls from the Philippines, like Aisha. All were pretty and well dressed and their hair and makeup was impeccable. Aisha felt she did not belong among so many beautiful girls, unaware of her own exquisite beauty. When she had said hello to everyone, Alina took her hand.

"Come; let's go get a glass of juice or something." She led Aisha to a table on the far wall where tea, juices, and water were laid out. An older woman served them. There seemed to be a servant for everything.

"Want an orange juice? It's fresh-pressed." Alina did not wait for Aisha's reply. She asked for two juices, and the maid poured them. Alina raised her glass. "Welcome to hell." Aisha looked at her perplexed, while taking a sip of her juice.

"Why do you say that, Alina? This place is so beautiful, it's like heaven. Aren't we just lucky to be here?" A frown adorned Aisha's face; the remark had disturbed her.

Alina did not answer; she led Aisha to where the other girls were standing about. "Look, I don't have time right now, but later, come by my room. We can drink tea and I will tell you all you need to know, ok?" She gave Aisha a reassuring smile. "Don't worry now, all will be fine, I'm just a bit sour today."

"Ok, Alina that would be great; let's do that later." She smiled too, feeling slightly less alarmed.

Just as they were mixing in with the girls, the doors that Aisha had come through with Mr. Za opened. A man came in; he was tall, dark, and very elegant. He wore a fine traditional robe made of silk with delicate gold trimmings. He held his head high and smiled to all, left and right. Slowly he made his way up to the podium and let himself sink into the numerous cushions. A servant came up to him bearing tea; he poured him some in a small tumbler type glass. The room was silent as if it was holding its breath. Mr. Za came up to him and bowed.

"Your Highness, I have a new guest to introduce to you, one which Mr. Chen has sent and that you have been expecting."

The Prince looked at Mr. Za straight in the eyes for a few seconds. "Very well, Mohamed, bring her up. I am anxious to meet this rare gem that that crook Chen has promised for so many years." The Prince was the only one who addressed Mr. Za by his first name.

"Yes Your Highness, at once." He backed away, bowing, and turned towards the girls and motioned to Aisha to come up the stairs.

Alina pushed Aisha forward. "Go now, it is time for your introduction. Don't worry, he won't bite."

Aisha moved forward through the girls towards Mr. Za. She climbed the steps of the podium, aware that every pair of eyes in the room was on her. She felt a slight tremor in her legs as she climbed up the steps. Mr. Za showed her the direction with his arm. She stood in front of the Prince. He looked her straight in the eyes. She blushed and turned her eyes to the floor and bowed as she had seen Mr. Za do just before.

"Your Highness, allow me to introduce your new guest, Miss Aisha Sayuno. She has been sent by Mr. Chen."

The Prince did not respond. He took his time, looking at Aisha from head to foot. She was a fine girl indeed, he concluded. He had noticed the grace with which she walked, and the fire in her eyes. "Magnificent," he thought, "absolutely magnificent, as fine as the finest unbroken stallion."

"Tell me child, how old are you?" His voice was soft and melodic. It put Aisha a little at ease.

Her answer was barely audible, as she had never spoken to a Prince before and she was intimidated.

"Seventeen and a half, Your Highness," Mr. Za had told her to always address the Prince as Your Highness.

"Did you enjoy your trip? Have you been well treated here? Have my people taken good care of you?" His concern for her well being seemed genuine and sincere and Aisha was touched by that.

"I have been very well treated, Your Highness, the trip was most exciting, thank you, and everyone has been most kind to me." Aisha was still staring at the floor.

"Good, I'm glad that all is well. In this house Aisha, you are my honored guest and you shall be treated as such. Is there anything that you wish to ask for, anything that I can do for you? You may look at me, girl." The Prince's voice had dropped to a near whisper.

Aisha raised her head. The Prince was smiling. "Such a handsome, kind man," she thought and she timidly smiled back.

"I only wish to start my education as soon as possible, Your Highness. I will be a good student, I promise. I am also anxious to write to my mother to tell her how lucky I am to be here in your care and under your protection."

The Prince was amused by her answer,

"Of course, Aisha, Mr. Za will help you settle in and get you organized. Your education is our main concern here. We will have the best for you, I will personally see to that."

"Thank you, Your Highness. I am most grateful, as is all my family for what you are doing for me."

"Think nothing of it, go now, join the other guests and feel at home, we will talk again, soon." Aisha smiled, bowed, and left the podium. The Prince motioned to Mr. Za to come closer. He whispered in his ear, "I approve strongly of Mr. Chen's choice. She is as promised, a rare beauty and an uncut diamond. Take extreme care of her Mohamed, she will be ready in a year or so and I consider her as a present from the almighty himself, understood?"

"Understood, you're Highness, I shall keep a special eye on her."

"Good, then let the entertainment begin and send me Gila and Fatma."

Mr. Za motioned to two girls who were very near the steps to come unto the podium. They were identical twins of twenty. Both had long, curly black hair that fell to their waists and the clothes they wore left no doubt about the perfect shapes of their bodies. They made their way sensually up the steps and went to sit on either side of the Prince. Each kissed one of his hands and leaned in his direction, love-filled eyes beaming towards him. Mr. Za clapped his hands and musicians appeared. The room was immediately filled with the mesmerizing music of Arabia. The voice of a man, coming from somewhere in the depths of the palace, accompanied the repetitive rhythm. Suddenly from the confines of the room, snake charmers and acrobats came running out and began to do their tricks. Some of the girls seemed bored, but most enjoyed the amusement. Aisha loved it. She was thrilled and excited; there was so much to see and absorb that her senses were overflowing from all the stimuli. Alina looked at her new friend, who was so pure and so happy. "Let's not spoil her fun," she thought, "not yet anyway."

A break came in the entertainment and Alina and Aisha went to sit on one of the numerous islands of cushions about the room. From where they sat, Aisha had a good view of the Prince on the podium. He now had his arms around the two girls. They were laughing and obviously having a great time.

"Which one is the Prince's wife, Alina?"

Alina choked on her juice. She coughed violently, grasping for air, and broke out laughing.

"I don't see what's so funny," Aisha was perplexed at her new friend's sudden outburst.

Catching her breath, Alina managed to say, "Oh it's nothing, Aisha, I just thought of something really funny, that's all. Now to answer your question, the Prince is not married and those two are the Turkish twins, Gila and Fatma. They are two little sluts, as far as I'm concerned, and the

Prince's current feminine amusement." Alina looked towards them with spite-filled eyes as she spoke. Aisha detected a taint of jealousy in her friend's voice.

"Well I guess that such a kind and generous man is allowed to do as he pleases." Aisha was trying to hide the fact that the word *slut* that Alina had used had shocked her. Alina turned to look at Aisha with a look of disbelief on her face.

"Don't worry, Aisha, the Prince only does as he pleases."

There was an awkward silence.

Alina decided to change the mood of her new friend, who had become gloomy all of a sudden. With her most cheerful voice she offered, "Hey, let's go to my room and have some tea and a talk, what do you say?"

"Yeah, ok, but are we allowed leaving like this? Won't the Prince be offended?"

"No he won't. You see, we have to come here every night for an hour or two, the nights that the Prince is in the palace, that is. Then we can leave if we so desire. Look around, some of the girls have left already." Aisha looked around; Alina was right. They got up and walked towards the large double doors. The white-clad guards opened the doors and let them by. Had Aisha noticed how the Prince looked at her as she left, she would have been surprised. His gaze was steady and intense. Fatma noticed though. She saw him look; she had seen that look before, but then the Prince had been looking at her. Her heart was instantly filled with hatred and jealousy for the newly arrived girl.

The girls walked down the endless, silent corridors, passing huge arches, gaudy decorations, and countless guards. The evening air was cool on their skin and Aisha felt better than she had ever felt in her life. For her, it was all unbelievable and fantastic; she had been brought to a world of pure enchantment and she felt that it was like a dream, but it wasn't made of dreams, it was real and she was living in it.

Alina's room was exactly like Aisha's, except the colors were bright and lively. Alina ordered tea and biscuits and the girls sat on the bed facing each other. Alina put on some music and Aisha stared at the mini sound system in amazement; she had never seen one before.

Alina responded to the gaze, thinking that it was the music that had provoked it.

"Music we're allowed," she said. "That's it, though, no television, no computers, no phones, and the radio around here you don't want to listen to, it's crap." The music was good; Aisha enjoyed it. It reminded her of music she had heard from cars stuck in traffic on the bridge above the underpass where she had lived. "If only Alina knew," she pondered, "in the world I grew up in, there were no computers or phones, or anything else."

The tea and biscuits arrived and Alina told Aisha her story. She was sixteen when she had arrived at the palace three years before. She was born in Moscow. Her mother had been a prostitute and a heroin addict.

"She told me my father was an American, but I never knew him. She said that they had been together for three years and that he was a diplomat of some sort. Just when she became pregnant with me, he left and returned to America and she never heard from him again. She did what she had to do to feed us. She told me the heroin helped make things bearable." Aisha listened in awe to her sad and pathetic story. It resembled her story in a lot of ways. Like her, she had known misery, hunger, and desperation. She went on to tell Aisha of the bitter cold winters in Moscow with no heating, of the cramped rooms they lived in, where her mother received her customers; who would more often than not beat her, because they were drunk or she was a junkie or both.

"I think I spent more time taking care of her, than she of me. Then one day, she died, just like that, drug overdose and one of my uncles took me in, Uncle Boris. I thought he was my savior, that old lying bastard." Alina was silent for a moment; Aisha did not dare speak, so absorbed she was in Alina's story.

"Well, good old Uncle Boris, he fed me and kept me for about a month or so. Then, one day, these two men arrived, they were of Middle Eastern origin, you know, Arabs, like here, and Uncle Boris told me, "Alina my child, I have arranged for you to have an education. These gentlemen will take you somewhere where good people will take care of you. I am old and alone, I cannot take care of a sixteen-year-old girl, this is for the best, believe me." He even shed a tear, the old bastard. Anyway, he told me he would write, that we would be in touch, that when I returned I would have a future and so on and so on. Well, the next thing you know, I end up here. I was sixteen, lost and very confused. As for Uncle Boris, I never heard from him again, to this day. I was like you when I arrived, you know. I thought it was heaven; it is in a way. It's beautiful, I am never cold, there is a roof over my head, there is plenty of food and just about everything that one may need. It took me awhile to realize what this place really is."

"What is it really, this place, Alina?" Aisha was worried again by her new friend's persistent negative insinuations about her new home.

Alina looked at Aisha, her eyes filled with sadness; her willingness not to spoil Aisha's fun as she had thought earlier had dissolved. "A prison, Aisha, that's what this place is, a prison."

"A prison, what do you mean by that, Alina?" Aisha was perplexed and alarmed.

"Ok, Aisha, take the guards for example, the ones dressed in white, they are the only guards who are allowed in the House of the Pure. Do you know why?"

Aisha shrugged "No," she answered.

"Well, they are all recruited in orphanages by Mr. Za. Actually he buys them, at a very young age. He then sends them to his training camp where they are castrated and put through a very extensive training or brainwashing program, whichever you prefer. They know nothing of the outside world, only what they are told or can remember. They are taught to obey Mr. Za instantly and without hesitation, even if the order is to kill someone. You see, they are brainwashed eunuchs, of no danger to us but a very real threat to anyone who comes near here and has no business doing so."

Aisha put her hand to her mouth. She was shocked by what she was hearing.

"Are you sure of this, Alina?" she asked in disbelief.

"Of course I am, and you know what else, these guards are intensely loyal and protective of this house and would not hesitate to die to save someone from getting hurt, including you. It is their purpose in life, to protect the Prince's women. The Prince does not allow anyone to come near his horses or his women. He is very possessive and jealous."

"What do you mean by his women, Alina? We are here to be educated in a strict and religious environment. I mean, the Prince told me so himself tonight. He said I would get the best education that he would see to it personally and…"

"Hush now, listen to me," Alina cut her off. Aisha's voice had begun to rise slightly from her growing concern. "You are a very young and very naïve girl. Your experience of the world is limited. You have to trust me when I tell you these things. I know what I'm talking about. You see, we are all the Prince's women. Oh, of course you will get your private tutors and teachers and everything else. But the real purpose we are here is to be ready for the Prince, if and when he decides that the time has come for you to be his."

"But that is just not possible, Alina. Mr. Chen promised me and Mama…"

"Mr. Chen, the Prince has ten Mr. Chens, all over the world Aisha. Their job is to find girls, young and pure girls like you, girls whose families are in dire situations and then, with the Prince's money, they buy out the family and convince them to send their girls here. Remember, Aisha, you belong to the Prince. To him you are like another expensive horse or rare thing that he's bought."

"Alina, all this is so incredible, it's almost unbelievable. Mama would not have sold me off, like a horse. She loves me; she would die for me and my sisters." Aisha shook her head in disbelief; she did not want to believe what Alina was telling her. "I am not and will never be one of the Prince's women," Aisha protested.

"Look, Aisha, I'm sure your mama is a good, loving person, but she is no match for the Mr. Chens of this world. But enough about this place and the Prince already, I see that it has troubled you and I'm sorry about that. You just got here and I shouldn't get you all confused about things. You'll figure things out on your own. Just forget what I told you for now, ok?" Aisha nodded her consent; she had heard enough for one day. "Now, I've told you my story, it's time for you to tell me yours. Tell me about your mama and your sisters. I want to know everything."

Although disturbed by what she had just heard, Aisha obliged her new friend and opened up to her. She told her everything, of her miserable upbringing in absolute, abject poverty and how inhospitable and ruthless life had been for her and her family, about her mother's big heart and about her sisters, the school, and the nuns and about her father's tragic death and the ensuing situation, which had forced her to quit school to take care of her sisters while her mother worked herself to death in a horrible factory. Then, how Mr. Chen showed up and with the money he gave her mother, it permitted them to survive and now, she was here.

"So you see, Alina, like you, I have not had an easy life. In my family, the love we have for each other is all we have. It is what unites us and keeps us together. That is something that no one can ever take from us. I miss them all so much you know." Aisha stared to the floor, saddened by the thought of her family so far away, and confused about what Alina had just told her.

Alina was touched by Aisha's story; it resembled the stories of most of the girls who were "guests" at the palace. She took Aisha's hand and wiped the tear that was rolling down her cheek. She took her in her arms and gave her a warm hug, as a big sister would have. "Oh come now, everything will be all right. I'll look out for you, I swear I will, ok?" Alina stroked Aisha's hair, and lifted her chin so their eyes could meet.

"Ok," she managed to say through her tears.

They smiled to each other, united by the bond of their newfound friendship.

Aisha did not sleep well that night. She tossed and turned in her bed. She woke up in the middle of the night and had trouble falling asleep again. She got out of bed around seven, sat at her desk, and wrote a long letter to her mother, telling her about the trip, the palace, and the Prince, leaving out everything that Alina had told her the night before. It was just too troubling, Aisha did not want to believe it and she certainly didn't want to worry her mother in any way.

There was a knock on her door and Aisha went to open it. It was Alina.

"Hi." Obviously she had slept well and was in high spirits. "Writing to someone?" she asked when she saw the letter on Aisha's desk.

"Yes, I wrote a letter to my mother, to tell her I'm fine and being well-treated."

"You have to give it to Mr. Za. He is responsible for all mail, in and out. Of course he will read it."

"What for, Alina?" Aisha was shocked.

"To make sure no one talks badly about the Prince or this place. The royal family is very sensitive as to how the outside world perceives them."

"But why would anyone want to do that, Alina? Everyone is well-treated, the place is wonderful."

"You'll see, Aisha, with time you will understand better. Just do as I say. I've been there, ok? Come now, get dressed and let's go get some breakfast." Aisha dropped the subject and got dressed.

The dining room was a very large, well-lit room situated at the extremity of one of the palace's many buildings. It could easily seat over one hundred people. A lot of the girls were already having breakfast. Every imaginable possibility of food was available. Aisha was stunned; she had never seen so much food in all her life.

"Wow, my family would live a long time on this." She stared at the long buffet tables, garnished with food. A chef was cooking eggs and omelets behind a counter nearby. She ordered one with cheese and ham. She loaded her plate with French toast, bacon, and just about everything else that was proposed. She sat down and began to devour her sizable plate.

"Hey, take it easy there. If you eat like this every day, you'll take fifty pounds; the Prince won't like that," Alina remarked sarcastically. Aisha licked her lips and leaned back. Her stomach was so full that she was unable to move.

"How do you know so much about the Prince, Alina?"

The answer she got was not the one she expected. "I was his favorite for nearly a year, until those two little Turkish bitches got their claws into him." Alina's voice was tainted with anger, her mood shifted.

"What do you mean his favorite?" Aisha ventured another question although she apprehended the answer.

"We were lovers, silly."

Aisha blushed. She was a virgin and had never even kissed a boy back home. It was not a subject that she wanted to elaborate on. She was intimidated by Alina's superior experience and maturity.

"Oh, I see," she said, sipping her juice loudly through a straw, hiding with difficulty her embarrassment. Sensing her discomfort, Alina decided to change the subject.

"Enough of this talk about the Prince; it seems to be all we talk about. So, what do you want to do today?"

Aisha was more than willing to change the subject. "I'd love to visit the school and meet some of the teachers."

Alina ignored Aisha's answer. "Hey I know what, I'll give you a grand tour of the palace, the grounds, the buildings, everything. What do you say?"

"Fine, I'd love to."

As they were leaving the dining room, Alina wanting to reassure her new friend added, "You don't have to worry about schooling, Aisha. We all have private teachers. Mr. Za will tell you how it works. He will do that in a few days. He will let you settle in first, you know, so you can adjust to the place."

"Ok, fine, I really appreciate all you're doing for me, Alina. Thank you for your kindness."

"Ah, come on, it's nothing, plus, we're friends now aren't we?"

"Yes, friends," Aisha smiled at her.

The girls spent the rest of the morning touring the palace. They visited the stables, pools, libraries, gyms, grounds and gardens. Everywhere there were servants, gardeners and guards. Not the white-clad ones of the House of the Pure, but the army-style ones that Aisha had seen on her arrival.

"How many people live and work here, Alina? It's so huge; it's like a city in itself."

"I'm not sure, but I heard that including everyone there are over two thousand people."

"Wow, the Prince must be very rich I guess."

"Filthy stinking rich would better describe it. His family has more money than they can spend in a thousand lifetimes."

Aisha learned from Alina during the tour that they were pretty well free to organize their time and activities as they wished. That is, with certain constraints, of course. They had to subscribe to a minimum of education, the minimum being two courses; the maximum was a full curriculum. The subjects taken were each individual's choice. Private teachers and tutors were provided in any given subject. The teachers and students dispensed courses at agreed-upon hours. A building served that purpose; it was fully equipped and very modern. The teachers were all foreigners, professionals and discreet, that had been selected and screened by the royal family. The rest of the time, the "guests" could choose from a vast variety of activities. Horseback riding, athletics, swimming, even shopping trips to the city's shopping centers, of course, exterior trips were strictly regulated. Bodyguards, limousines were a must. The girls also had to wear the traditional robes and put a veil over their face. The only real obligation they had was to be present every evening in the Prince's parlor if he was in the palace. They also had to attend any celebration or birthday party that the Prince organized. The girls had to dress at their best and be of pleasant and agreeable disposition at all times in his presence. The Prince had the habit of throwing a birthday party for every girl on her birthday. He always gave the birthday girl a piece of expensive jewelry. Every girl received fifty dollars a week that she could save, send to her family, or spend on a future shopping trip. Aisha decided she would send all her money to her mother. Aisha learned a lot on those first few days with Alina. She did not mind that they did not have access to television, movies, or that all outside communication was blocked off. It was a situation that really upset Alina, however.

"Mr. Za will tell you that it is to preserve out purity," Alina warned, "but its' all bullshit Aisha, they just want to keep us ignorant of what's going on in the world. The most important rule you have to remember is that no man in this palace, guard, servant, or gardener, none are allowed to speak to you, unless you speak to them first. The guards of the House of the Pure are not even allowed to look at us directly, as you have probably noticed. The exception to this rule is Mr. Za; if he should catch a man trying to engage in informal conversation with any one of us, he would immediately be sent away, a disgrace to his family. I even heard that depending on what the culprit said, or who the girl was, the man could be whipped, jailed, and even executed. The Prince's "guests" are for his exclusive enjoyment and companionship." The last sentence she said in a voice that imitated Mr. Za's deep, raspy voice. Both girls broke out laughing.

"Be careful, Alina, someone could hear us," Aisha scolded her through the laughter.

Alina brushed off the warning. "So you see you won't have to worry about boys or falling in love here. It's impossible, unless you fall in love with the Prince. Now, that is permitted."

"I don't care. I came here to get educated, not to fall in love, plus I will be able to send money home to my mother. The Prince does not need me, he has all the women he wants, so I will quietly go about my affairs and I intend to have a marvelous and productive time here."

Alina said nothing. Aisha was young and inexperienced; she knew that her education laid in the near future, her real one that is.

So Aisha settled into the luxurious life of the palace. She took as many courses as it was possible to take and cram into her weekly schedule. She was a very hard-working and dedicated student. She spent every spare moment of her time working on her studies. Her appetite for knowledge was limitless. Her brilliance and intelligence impressed all of her teachers and tutors. Her educational zeal frustrated her new friend, Alina, who thought that Aisha did not allot enough time to have some genuine "girl time." Aisha ignored her friendly scolding and carried on with her furiously busy program.

Aisha wrote to her mother every week. She would always include in the envelope forty dollars of her fifty-dollar allowance money. She kept the other ten dollars for a future shopping trip, at which time she would buy clothes or utility items that she would send home. Her mother wrote to her about once a month.

"It's normal," thought Aisha, "after all, she's so busy and to send a letter is a special trip to the post office that she has to do on her day off. Through her mother's letters, she got news from home. It was the most exciting time of the month for her; to know that all her sisters were well and that the money she sent made life easier for them and that they all loved her very much and missed her a lot. Her mother would sometimes include some drawings that she had the little ones draw for her. She would hang them up in her room; it touched Aisha's heart to see those drawings and it made her feel less homesick.

So Aisha's fairy tale life at the palace continued uninterrupted. It was like living on another planet. She studied, ate well, occasionally went horseback riding with Alina, or swam in one of the many pools. But mostly, she devoured every book she could get her hands on. It was the happiest time of her young life. She did not mind the evenings in the Prince's parlor. It was a good place to chat with some of the girls and a lot of them had become friends. The Prince paid no particular attention to her, or she to him.

So the first year that she spent at the palace flew by with enchantment. Life was good and sweet. During the course of that year, Aisha had blossomed into a magnificent young woman. She was now eighteen and a half and her features had sharpened and her body had grown. The Prince began to notice her growing beauty; his gaze was constantly straying towards her when she was in the parlor. He was becoming more and more attracted to her. He saw how she stuck out in the crowd of girls. She was a good head or so taller than the others, bearing herself with grace and elegance. Her very presence created a stir and seemed to ignite the immediate area around her. He had followed her evolution through Mr. Za, who had kept him informed of her progression.

"Soon, my little desert flower, soon, you will be mine, all mine." The Prince's thoughts caused his manhood to stir as he observed her from his podium one evening. Aisha didn't notice his growing interest for her. The other girls did, however; it was becoming more and more obvious by the day.

It was at about that time that Aisha stopped receiving letters from her mother; it had been more than two months since she had received a letter and she was getting more and more worried. "Mr. Chen should be coming soon," she thought. "I hope he has news." Every day she went to see Mr. Za and every day he said the same thing, "Sorry, no mail for you today." Aisha would walk away, downtrodden and eaten by anxiety.

"It's nothing Aisha; she's probably too tired or too busy to write. Hey, look at it this way, no news good news, ok." Alina held her by the shoulders and was trying hard to cheer her up. "Come on now, lift that head up, there you go, that's better now." Aisha managed a smile to please her friend, but her heart was heavy with a growing sense of desperation. Every day, her fears and anxieties grew worse.

Her recent conversations with Mohini did not help at all. Ever since the first day Aisha had arrived, they had liked each other. Mohini was responsible to provide room service for about ten girls in Aisha's wing of the House of the Pure. Mohini was about the age of Aisha's mother and had six children of her own back home. She sent all the money she earned to her husband and her mother so they could take care of themselves and the children. She had been working for the Prince for ten years. Twice a year, she went home for three weeks. She had become like a second mother to Aisha. She took care of her as if she were her own daughter. They talked at night when Mohini brought Aisha some tea. She would always serve her last, so they could spend some time together. Lately, as she had become aware of Aisha developing into a beautiful young woman, she had talked a lot to her about men and women, in their intimate relations. Aisha was embarrassed by this subject and had protested.

"But Mohini, I will not take a husband soon, not here anyway. I will have time for these things later, there is no hurry."

"Hush, child, it is time that you know the most important things a woman must know, trust me, please." So Aisha had listened to her more out of respect for Mohini than for any real interest in the subject.

Mohini had another subject that she would bring up more often and that was the Prince. In the ten years she had been at the palace, she had seen and witnessed a lot.

"You must be very careful, my child," Mohini whispered, looking about to make sure no one was listening, "he will consume you like fire consumes wood, believe me, I have seen it many times with my own eyes."

"But Mohini, he doesn't even look at me, you're imagining things." Aisha had lowered her voice to a whisper too.

"Oh no, I'm not, I know these things. I see how he looks at you, with the eyes of a starving wolf that has spotted his prey. He has seen you and he will come for you, mark my words."

"It's so silly, Mohini, the Prince has all the women he wants; he does not need me." Aisha was by now wise to the fact that most of the girls had either slept with the Prince, were still doing so, or hoped to do so soon. The Prince was very generous with his favorite girls, covering them with gifts and jewelry. The competition to be his favorite was very intense in the parlor. It was a competition that Aisha did not participate in. Her only objective was to get an education and to send money to her family. The thought that the Prince had taken notice of her secretly pleased her, however. Her... Aisha Sayuno... a poor girl from the most humble of origins, was being noticed by a Prince. It was a flattering and ego boosting thought for the romantically disillusioned young virgin that she was.

Her friend Alina sang the same song about the Prince as Mohini, except her words were much harsher, "Ah, but you underestimate our royal horniness my dear." She spoke softly so that no one could overhear. "He has an unquenchable appetite for women, especially young and inexperienced ones like you."

Aisha said nothing. She knew that Mohini and Alina were right about the Prince, his sexual appetite was the main subject of conversation in the parlor... all the girls discussed it continuously. Secretly in her young and inexperienced heart, she hoped the Prince was in love with her. She found him to be a very handsome and attractive man; also he was rich and a Prince, which were most certainly big pluses.

"I would make my conditions," she would say to herself as she lay in her bed at night, pondering the subject. "I will say to him, ok, I will be your wife forever, but I must be the only one, no more other women." She would imagine the

Prince, carried by his love for her, falling on his knees and saying, "Yes, my Aisha, love of my life, I accept your conditions and tomorrow I shall send them all home. I also promise you that I will be only with you for the rest of my life, if you would only accept to marry me." She would then lift him from his knees and say to him, "Yes I will marry you and be your Princess," and then they would kiss passionately for a very long time. Then she dreamed of returning home with her husband the Prince and introducing him to her mother and sisters. Of course the Prince would build them a comfortable home with everything inside that they needed to make their life pleasant and good. Thus she dreamed of her relationship with the Prince, her naïveté was absolute.

"Just remember, my little Aisha," Mohini continued, "he is a very powerful man. You are under his control, he does not understand or accept people who do not do as he wishes, especially a woman. Be obedient; do not question his will or his wants. He has been known to have fits of violent behavior." She spoke the last sentence in a whisper, while looking about for indiscreet ears.

"Six years ago he beat a girl so badly she spent two months in the hospital. Believe me, child, the Prince can be very unpleasant."

Aisha listened gravely to all these confidences and warnings from Mohini, but inhabited with the fearlessness of youth, she remained convinced that she could handle the Prince. "After all," she told herself, "he was a civilized and educated man, he would understand, if he loved her."

She confided in Mohini her concerns about being without news from her family for over two months. She also mentioned that Mr. Za had told her not to worry because sometimes there were problems with the mail. The very mention of Mr. Za's name made her jump, every time his name came up. Mohini feared and loathed him intensely.

Ever since Aisha's arrival, she had warned her constantly about Mr. Za.

"He is a villain and a scoundrel and a snake of the worst kind; do not trust him for a second, he is a vicious and wicked man," she would hiss. "Stay away from him, I beg you, be most careful," she would add with the utmost gravity. "I wouldn't be surprised if he hid the letters from your mother himself just to torture you, that insect." Mohini was getting upset, as always when Mr. Za's name was mentioned.

"Why would he do that, Mohini? He has no cause or reason to." The older woman looked at Aisha with a fierce look, locking eyes with her.

"Because he is an evil man, my child, and evil men such as him do evil things, things that you cannot even imagine. You must be very careful of him. Always be cautious and on your guard."

"I will, Mohini, I promise." Aisha wanted to calm her down as she was very agitated. "I will be careful and I will heed all of your warnings, ok?"

"Good, very good," Mohini got up. "I must go now, my child, get some rest, good night."

"Good night, my dearest Mohini, thank you for the tea and your company."

"It's nothing, sweet dreams now." Mohini picked up the tray with the remains of the tea and biscuits and let herself out of Aisha's room. She walked quickly down the long, silent corridors with a deep frown on her face, worried about Aisha, this magnificent child who had been sent to her to watch over. When she reached the door of the kitchen quarters, she turned and looked up to the star-studded sky and whispered under her breath, "Oh almighty one, I beg of you, please spare her, please."

A week later, Aisha asked to speak to Mr. Za about a private matter.

"I will come to see you later," he had replied, without emotion.

"Thank you, Mr. Za." Aisha's plan was to try to convince him to help her get in contact with her family, or at least to get some news. She was worried sick about them. Mr. Za was a powerful man, surely he could help her. She had put aside all of Mohini's warnings about him. Her only concern was for her mother and sisters.

"Mr. Za had always been very polite and nice to me for the past year or so," she reflected. "What was there to fear, there were guards everywhere, the other girls, not to mention the Prince? Nothing could happen to me. Mohini is just too overprotective and sees evil everywhere," she concluded.

That evening at about nine-thirty, Aisha was in her room studying when someone knocked at her door. She opened the door; it was Mr. Za.

"Good evening Mr. Za, please, won't you come in?" She stepped aside and he let his huge person in. "Would you like some tea, sir? It is fresh and warm."

"Yes, thank you." He sat down on one of the elegant couches.

He put the teacup to his lips and drained it in one gulp. He put the cup down and looked over to Aisha with his bulging bloodshot eyes. "Now, tell me girl, what is this urgent matter that you wish to speak to me about in private?"

"Well, Mr. Za, it's about my mother and sisters. I am very concerned about them. I have had no news in over two months, as you know, and it's driving me crazy. I was hoping you could help me in this matter, considering your power and influence." Aisha's voice was laden with anguish and anxiety. Mr. Za sat silent for a moment, reflecting on what he would say.

"I see, now don't you think you are being alarmed for nothing, as I've told you before, there are problems sometimes with mail delivery or maybe they just haven't written to you, I don't know." He shrugged his large shoulders to emphasize his words.

"Oh no, Mr. Za, that is simply not possible. My mother would never stop writing to me. We are very close. Something is wrong, I can feel it." Aisha crossed the room and fell to her knees in front of him. "Please, Mr. Za, I beg you, please help me, I am so worried." Tears rolled down her cheeks.

"Come, come, girl." He wiped the tears on her face with his big, callous hands. "Let's not get this way now. Mr. Za will see what he can do, I will contact Mr. Chen and surely he can give us news of your family."

"Oh thank you, Mr. Za, thank you so much." Aisha took one of his hands and kissed it, holding onto it tightly.

"Ok now." Mr. Za helped her up from the floor. "Come now, let's sit you back down." He helped her regain her chair and went back to sit on the sofa. "Now, there are conditions that you must respect if you wish me to intervene on your behalf."

"I'll do whatever you say, Mr. Za, I promise."

"Good, now the first thing is that this matter must remain strictly between you and I. This is very important. If you speak to anyone about my involvement, I will deny it and that will be the end of it. I do not want all the girls to come to me with special requests. Is that clear?"

"Of course sir, very clear, this is a private matter between us, I shall be eternally grateful and silent, I promise." Aisha had regained her composure; she felt better and would have accepted any condition that Mr. Za would impose.

"Very well then, as for the other conditions, I will tell you those at a later time, but for now, all I ask is absolute, total silence." Mr. Za set his gaze on her for a few seconds to make sure that his words had sunk in.

"Yes sir, absolute silence, I promise."

Mr. Za got up. "Very well then, get some rest, girl. I will look into this in the next few days, good night now."

"Good night sir and thank you again for your kindness."

"Yes, yes, fine," Mr. Za said as he closed the door of her room behind him and began to walk to his quarters. He smiled as he walked away.

"The lamb is nearly ready," he thought, "soon Mohamed; soon you will be rewarded for keeping those letters. Ha, ha," he laughed out loud to himself, as he walked down the long silent carpeted corridors.

Three nights later, Mr. Za came to see Aisha again, at about the same time. She let him in.

"You have spoken to no one about our last conversation, now have you?" He towered over her, projecting by his height and weight a threatening vibration.

"But of course not sir," she protested defensively, "never, I would never speak to anyone about anything, as we agreed, I promise on my mother's life, I have spoken to no one."

"Very well then, let us sit down and talk." He indicated for her to sit on the sofa and he sat down beside her. His proximity made her feel uneasy.

Instead of telling her about her family, Mr. Za began to tell her about how hard he worked, that it was a twenty-four seven job, which offered no time off. The Prince, he confided, was a very generous employer but also very difficult. The price he had paid to keep this job had been extreme loneliness. He had no family, no friends, nothing. Aisha did not fully comprehend where Mr. Za was going with this conversation, but she did not want to appear uninterested or insensitive. She listened patiently and politely, nodding her understanding and sympathy. After thirty minutes or so, Mr. Za leaned forward towards her and half whispered, "You know, we could help each other. I could help you with your problem and you could help me with mine, what do you say?"

The abruptness of the question caught Aisha off guard.

"But how could I help you, sir? I am just a poor student who has no money or power," Aisha feigned confusion, as if she did not quite understand what Mr. Za was talking about.

"Oh, but you can girl. I will show you how you can help me. It is easy, you will see, the only condition being, once again, total, absolute, silence. You must talk to no one about our little secrets, especially not to that woman Mohini, whom you have befriended. No one, do you understand?"

"Of course, Mr. Za., but I…"

He cut her off with a movement of his hand. "Hush now, you will understand later." Aisha was silenced by his tone and her growing fear about what was to come.

"First, let me tell you about your family." This caught her attention. "I spoke to Mr. Chen. Something seems to have happened." He let the words sink in.

Aisha's heart sank, she put her hand to her mouth, "Oh, my God."

"No, no, do not worry, they are all alive and well. It's just some kind of trouble, money trouble your mother seems to have gotten into. Mr. Chen could not give me details, there were people with him when we spoke and the connection was bad. He could not speak freely but he said he would call me in two or three days. I will know more at that time."

"But what is this trouble that my mother got into, Mr. Za? I don't understand, what can I do to help?" Aisha's anxiety was as intense as was her relief to know that her mother and sisters were all well.

"Nothing for now, we must wait, we will know more in a few days. You must be patient, everything will be ok, do not worry; Mr. Za will see to it."

He reached over to her and stroked her forearm. His hands were rough on her tender skin. Aisha felt a shudder of dread pass through her spine. She wanted to remove her arm, but did not dare. He leaned forward again. "Now go lock the door and I will show you how you can help me."

Trembling and in a state of shock, Aisha got up and obeyed. She was in a trance and kept saying to herself that the only thing that mattered was her family, whatever the price she would have to pay. She was ready yet terrified about what would happen next. She locked the door and turned to face Mr. Za.

"Come and sit over here beside me." He motioned to the place she had been sitting before. She did as he asked, sitting rigid and tense, staring at the thickly carpeted floor.

"Relax girl, do not be afraid. Mr. Za will not hurt you; he only wants to appease his loneliness." His tone was gentle and soft. He took her hand and guided it under his robe to his exposed penis. He began to masturbate himself with her hand, putting his head back, eyes closed. Aisha was shaking from head to foot. Very quickly he had an orgasm. He moaned and groaned and it frightened Aisha, thinking he had become ill or something. She wanted to remove her hand but he held it firmly. After a few moments he opened his eyes, and smiled,

"You see, that was not so difficult? Now go get a hot towel and clean me up." He had regained his authoritarian tone. "Come on, girl, on with it."

Aisha did as she was told. She cleaned him with a hot towel, trying not to touch him with her hands. He rose when she was done.

"I will see you in few days, just remember, silence," he looked at her intensely. "Think of your family," the latter being said as a threat.

"Yes sir." She bowed and stared to the floor, unable to look at him because she was so ashamed of what had just happened.

As soon as he was gone, Aisha ran to the bathroom and washed her hands repeatedly, hoping to scrub away Mr. Za's vileness. She had never felt so ashamed in all her life. She could not help but think how right Mohini had been about Mr. Za and how she apprehended what was to come. She slept very badly that night, twisting and turning in her bed, until the wee hours of the morning.

The next day she rationalized the situation. "It is for my family," she thought, "to save them." It became her motivation and she decided that from then on no matter what, she would be detached from whatever happened with Mr. Za.

It was about that time that the Prince began to make his attraction for Aisha more and more obvious. He could not ignore her immense beauty and poise any longer. Mr. Za had kept the Prince well informed of her evolution. He knew that she was a serious student, that all her teachers and tutors praised her intelligence and devotion to her studies. He also knew that she was very loyal to her family and that she sent all of her allowance money to them, never buying anything for herself. But mostly the Prince had noticed how everyone was drawn to her. She was like a people magnet; the girls in the parlor, the servants, all sought her company and friendship. He had been observing her and now he wanted her and his desire grew by the day. He summoned Mr. Za to his quarters and he arrived flushed and out of breath.

"Your Highness has called for me?"

"Yes Mohamed, tonight I wish that Aisha sit with me. She has grown worthy of my attention. I am tired of Parveen; she is so immature and has nothing of any interest to say. Tonight, you bring me Aisha. Last night I dreamt about her, Mohamed. It is a sign, you know, a sign from the almighty himself."

"Yes Your Highness, I agree, it shall be done as you request. Is there anything else, Your Highness?"

"No Mohamed, that will be all, you may go."

"Very well, you're Highness." Mr. Za bowed again and left precipitously, leaving the Prince to his divine inspirations.

Aisha was sitting alone on a bench, lost in her thoughts. Alina walked up to her, dressed in a tennis uniform, dangling a tennis racket by her side.

"Hey, what's up?"

"Not much and you?"

Alina had noticed how depressed Aisha had been lately. She thought it was out of concern for her family.

"My tennis game is getting good and I would love to go shopping, want to come?"

"No thanks, you know I don't go shopping."

"Yeah, but I thought it might cheer you up; you've been so moody lately. Look, Aisha, I know you're concerned about your family, but you told me you had had news and that they were ok, right?"

"Yes."

"So stop worrying, will you? So look, I'll tell you what. I want you to come with me. You don't have to buy anything, but you could help me choose my clothes, what do you say? Oh come on, it'll be fun. I just won't take no for an answer this time. You're coming and that's it." Alina's plea struck a sensitive chord with Aisha, who gave in, more to please her friend than for herself.

"Ok, I'll go. I've never been, so it will be a new experience, right?"

"Great, I'm glad, so let's meet at the limousine garage in about forty-five minutes. I'll go get permission from Mr. Za." The very mention of his name made Aisha's heart turn upside down.

"Ok, I'll be there," Aisha said without much conviction. Without further discussion, Alina ran off towards the House of the Pure, happy to have her friend along with her and hoping it would cheer her up.

Aisha just sat there, a heavy weight upon her shoulders. The abuse of Mr. Za had gotten worse lately. He came to see her at least once a week. Fifteen or twenty minutes after Mohini had left he would knock at her door and let himself in. He gave her news of her family, but it was always fragmented, making sure that she understood that he and Mr. Chen held their lives in their hands and that any mistake she made would be fatal to all of them. He would repeat what he always told her, that he and Mr. Chen were working on straightening things out for her mother and he would add that it was very difficult and she should thank them for the trouble they were giving themselves and that it would require that they pull a lot of strings and it would cost a lot of money. He also assured her that Mr. Chen would visit soon and bring her fresh news and letters. He never explained the exact nature of Aisha's mother's problems. It was all very unclear and confusing to Aisha, so she believed him, because she had nothing else to hang on to. His continuing abuse of her was very clear, however. It was degrading and humiliating and it made her physically sick. Every time when he was done, Aisha would run to the bathroom and vomit. When she returned with a pale face, Mr. Za would say, "Really girl, you should not act like that, you should be happy with what I give you so generously."

Aisha was too sick and repulsed to answer his usual tirade. Before he left, he always repeated the same warning. "Do not forget, if you want your family to live, our little arrangement must remain a secret to all." The way he pronounced the threat left no doubt in Aisha's mind that he would not hesitate to have her family killed if she did not do what he asked or if she told a single soul about it. So, she bore her horrible secret alone and it slowly ate away at her soul.

"Look at these people, it's unbelievable, it's like living in the Middle Ages, the women all veiled and treated like children or cattle, its' incredible." Alina was staring out the limousine window. They were going through the old part of the city, with its narrow meandering streets, filled with people and vendors of all sorts. The limo had tinted windows so no one outside could see them and there was a window that separated them from the driver and the bodyguard sitting up front. It was a strange feeling to be in this air-conditioned car, in complete privacy and in the middle of the pandemonium outside.

"No one is even looking at the car, isn't that strange? Why do you think that is, Aisha?"

"They must know it is a car which belongs to the royal family. In a country like this, it is better to mind one's own business, especially in matters which concern the royal family."

Aisha was also staring through the car window to the bustling scene outside. She was looking at the people, mostly the women, who were veiled and walked quickly in groups of twos or threes, eyes furtively looking about or staring to the ground. It was then that Aisha realized two things; the first being that she had not stepped outside the palace grounds in over a year and the second was that she was developing a profound hatred for this country, its people, and its ways. It was a new sentiment for her, since tolerance and love of all had always been the guiding lights of her young, emotional life.

"Yeah, I guess you're right about that, people here must stay clear of anything that has to do with the royal family, I can understand that. I mean they own this place, heart and soul, they have power of life or death over any living soul, so I guess that commands caution."

Suddenly the car turned right and took a larger street which led them to a highway. They sped along it for about ten miles or so and outside there was nothing but desert. They came up to a huge, modern, and obviously brand new shopping center. The car pulled up to the front doors of the large mall. The chauffeur and bodyguard got out, and each one opened a door for the girl on his side of the car. Both girls had put on their veils, as instructed by Mr. Za. It was the only condition imposed on them if they went shopping. They entered the huge, air-conditioned building. The place was immense, sprawling in every direction, full of everything under the sun. The only things that there were not much of were shoppers. The girls had a great time, with the two black-suited men always a few feet behind them. They bought some shoes and trinkets and two very pretty dresses.

Alina asked Aisha to try the dresses on, but she refused.

"Oh, come on, Aisha, I want to see what they'll look like on me, please." The girls were practically the same size. So, Aisha had tried them on to please Alina. Of the two she tried on, there was a baby blue satin dress with a low back, which looked stunning on her. She looked at herself in the mirror, liking the effect of the dress. Alina came up behind her.

"It looks fabulous on you, the Prince will love it."

"Why would he notice? Anyway, this dress is not for me, it's for you." Aisha turned to face her friend, whose smile said, "I know something you don't know."

Aisha looked at her perplexed. "Well, what?"

"That dress is for you, Aisha, and the Prince will notice it when you sit with him tonight. Mr. Za told me before we went shopping that the Prince has requested that you sit with him tonight."

"Are you serious, Alina? Did he really say that?"

"I swear to God, those are his very words, plus he gave me three hundred dollars to buy you some new clothes."

Aisha was stunned. She had both feared and anticipated this moment, now it all appeared so sudden.

"What shall I do, Alina?"

"You shall wear that dress, those new shoes, do your hair and makeup, and then you shall sit with the Prince. What else is there to do?"

"Of course, yes, it's just that it's a bit of a shock, I don't know what to think, or how to act. Will you help me, Alina?"

"Yes, I'll help you, silly. Don't worry, you'll get over it, everything will be fine, you'll see. I can't wait to see the face of that little whore Parveen tonight. Oh, that will be fun and pleasure, I can't wait."

"Don't be so mean, Alina, and watch your language, please."

"I'm sorry, so, come on let's go, we have to get you ready for tonight."

The girls spent the rest of the day in Aisha's room talking and preparing for the evening.

"How was he, Alina, how was the Prince?" Aisha asked hesitantly.

"You mean, as a man?"

"Yeah, I guess so."

"Well he is normal, you know, with a woman that is. He can be very tender and kind, but also very aggressive. He has a violent temper. Never disagree with him, it is not done, you understand?"

"I understand," Aisha nodded solemnly.

"Do not try to be smarter than him, let him lead the conversation, show interest in what he says, laugh at his jokes. Let him decide what happens, you follow me?"

"Yes Alina, I follow you. I'm scared, that's all. I've never been with a man before, ever."

"Oh, don't worry, things will work out, you'll see." She paused from brushing Aisha's hair. "Look, I'll be nearby if you need me, ok?"

"Ok, thanks Alina, I appreciate that."

"Hey, that's what friends are for." Aisha could not see Alina's face because she was behind her again, brushing her hair. If she had, she would have seen the deep frown on her face. Alina was concerned for her; she had known the Prince and his violent temper. She did not share her thoughts with Aisha however; who she figured had enough on her mind.

That evening, Aisha and Alina arrived last in the Prince's parlor. They wore their new dresses and were strikingly beautiful. The other girls took notice, particularly of Aisha, who was never this done up. The doors opened and the Prince entered, and Aisha's body was overtaken by a slight tremor. The Prince did his usual thing about the room. The music began and soon he was comfortably installed in his mountain of cushions on the podium. Immediately, a servant came up and poured him a tumbler of tea. He gave a signal to Mr. Za. Parveen, who was near the steps, began to move, but Mr. Za motioned to her not to move with an outstretched hand. With the other, he signaled to Aisha to come forward. Aisha walked slowly through the crowd of girls, to the sound of the exotic Arabian music, her heart beating fast, passing a stunned Parveen. Elegantly she walked up the few steps of the podium, looking straight into the Prince's eyes, inhabited by the unshakeable confidence of youth, sure that she could "win this thing." The Prince smiled and motioned for her to sit. She took off her shoes and sat beside him, without unlocking her eyes on his, she smiled back, placing her dress about her legs, and said, "Thank you, Your Highness, I am honored to sit with you."

"I am glad that you are here, Aisha. You have grown into the brightest star of my universe. Your beauty is great and unique and I am deeply touched by it." He put his hand on his chest and bowed slightly in a gesture of respect.

Aisha lowered her eyes and blushed. She was thrilled by the compliment, but she quickly regained her adroitness. "Thank you, Your Highness, I find you to be a very handsome man yourself, if I may say so, Your Highness."

Her assurance and poise amused the Prince. "You may, Aisha and I thank you for the compliment."

So the evening went, passing very quickly, inundated with music, incense, and tea. The two were oblivious to anyone else around. Aisha told the Prince of her studies, and he listened, amused. For him, the education of women was a waste of time, but he kept his thoughts to himself. Aisha's beauty, her eyes, her lips, her hair, everything about her was so perfect, it mesmerized him, she was a rare beauty and he loved rare and beautiful things. He would take his time with this one. There was no hurry. "This is one to be consumed slowly, as a delicacy," he concluded to himself.

The Prince was very charming and articulate; he told Aisha about his family and his passion for horses and falcons. His favorite bird, he told her, was called "blue eye." He was called so because by a freak of nature, he had one blue and one brown eye.

"I would love to see your birds, Your Highness." Aisha followed Alina's instructions well.

"It would be my pleasure to have you along. I was planning on visiting them tomorrow and to have some of them fly. I will send for you in the afternoon."

"Fine, I look forward to it, Your Highness." Aisha knew she would have to cut a few courses, but now was not the time to bring that up.

They had been talking for over three hours and the room was practically empty, when the Prince said, "you must be tired now and you study early tomorrow morning, you should go to bed now, come, I will walk with you to your room."

Aisha was happy he suggested this, as she was a bit tired from all the emotions of the day. She rose and accompanied the Prince down the steps towards the door. As they were about to leave the room, the Prince motioned to Mr. Za to approach. He leaned towards the Prince, who said something to him in his ear. Mr. Za nodded and bowed to the Prince. As soon as Aisha and the Prince were out the door, Mr. Za motioned to a girl sitting in a far corner of the room by herself to come to him. She was Parveen, the Prince's current female companion and was a tall elegant girl of eighteen from Pakistan. Her skin was café crème and her eyes were an incredible mix of green and yellow. Everybody liked Parveen, except Alina that is. She was a sweet and soft-spoken girl and she lowered her eyes when she came up to Mr. Za.

"Go to the Prince's chambers now. He will join you shortly." He motioned to a guard the direction of the Prince's chambers and he quickly followed Parveen in the direction that she knew quite well. In the exchange with Mr. Za, she had said nothing, she had obeyed, silently, submissively; it was what was expected of her and she understood that well.

Aisha and the Prince walked slowly down the corridors of the House of the Pure. "Are you happy here?" the Prince asked.

"Yes Your Highness, very much so." Aisha bit her lip; she wished she could tell him about her concern for her family and the horrible things that Mr. Za did to her, but she knew that she had to keep silent or her family's life could be at risk.

"Good, I'm glad to hear that." They arrived at her door; the Prince and Aisha stood facing each other. Aisha was very nervous about what could happen next. The Prince took her hand and kissed it. "So, I will see you tomorrow afternoon?"

Relieved that he was not being abrupt with her, Aisha answered, "Yes, Your Highness, I look forward to it very much."

"Good and thank you for the wonderful evening. I hope there will be many more of them, I enjoy your company immensely."

"So do I, Your Highness, good night then." As she turned to enter her room, she smiled to him before closing the door and he smiled back. She sat on the edge of the bed awhile, motionless, her heart palpitating wildly. She was excited and scared at the same time.

"He loves me," she thought, "he loves me, he loves me." She got up and danced about the room. It was a new and strange emotion, and it inhabited her completely. "A Prince," she kept turning the phrase in her head, "a Prince is in love with me and I shall be a Princess." A sudden rapping on her door interrupted her naïve, romantic reveries.

Her heart sank as she opened the door. It was Mr. Za who let himself in and went to sit on the sofa. She closed and locked the door behind him.

"You did well tonight. My master approves of you and that is a good thing, but, you must never forget Mr. Za and his kindness to you and your family." His gaze directed at her was intense and laden with menace. "If you open your mouth, they are all dead, you understand me, girl? I have given instructions."

"Yes, I understand, Mr. Za, I will never say a word to anyone, as I have promised, just do not hurt my family, that's all that I ask."

In response Mr. Za lifted his robe, exposing himself. "Good then, now come and relieve me of my loneliness, I am much in need tonight." He leaned his head back and waited for her to obey.

Meanwhile, the Prince had joined Parveen in his chambers. She had bathed and lay naked on his oversized bed. Her perfect coffee-colored body shone, reflecting the light of over a hundred candles. The Prince undressed, came to lie beside her, and began to caress her soft skin.

"Ah my little Pakistani angel, I have been thinking of you for days, for days I have dreamt of your taste in my mouth." He kissed her passionately, and she returned his embrace. Parveen was a smart girl; she knew the gestures and the moves; she knew her place. They made love quickly and violently. The Prince imagined it was Aisha he was taking and the thought made him strong. Parveen responded to his every thrust with vigor and passion. When he was done, she pretended to have an orgasm, as usual. The Prince rolled over on his back. "Ah, it was good for you too my little angel?" he looked over towards her.

She looked at him, her eyes full of what he wanted to see. Parveen was a survivor; she had been raised in misery, and it had made her smart.

"Oh, Your Highness, it was as if a river of love had swept me away. I am still shaken by its strength and power."

"Me too, it was the same." He closed his eyes satisfied with his virility and power. Soon he was snoring loudly. Parveen lay with her eyes open, staring at the ceiling, unable to sleep, as usual.

The next morning, Aisha told Alina about her evening with the Prince. She was so excited, Alina couldn't believe how adolescent and childish she was.

"I think he loves me, Alina."

"Yeah, sure, he loves us all, you idiot."

"No, I mean it, I can feel it here." She pointed to her gut. "I think I love him too, well, I'm not one hundred percent sure yet, but I feel something for him."

"Oh shit, you're such a fool, Aisha. Come on; let's go get some breakfast. I've heard all I can for now." She rose and went to her room to get dressed. Aisha just sat there, dreaming about her and the Prince, as husband and wife, with two or three royal children, madly in love, forever and ever. All the other girls were finished; he would be only with her. As for Mr. Za, she would settle her scores with him when it was time, the Prince would see to that. Alina poked her head in the doorway.

"Hey, come on, lover girl, I'm hungry." Aisha ignored her comment. She got up and slowly got dressed, her whole being warmed by her dreams. Later that morning, she asked the head tutor to be taught Arabic. She thought that it was important that she learn the language, if she was to be the Prince's wife.

During the course of the next few days, Alina came to realize how much her friend was in dire need of a wake-up call about the Prince. She undertook to tell Aisha of her own tumultuous eight-month relationship with the Prince.

"He was great at the beginning, polite and friendly and I fell for it, its' a bit ridiculous when you think of it though, I mean, considering that fifty women surround the man and are at his disposal. Anyway, it felt good to be the one he had chosen, I felt special and important.

He was actually nice for quite a while, then for the slightest of reasons he would explode. He is very violent, Aisha, believe me, I saw it up close and personal."

"Did he hurt you?" Aisha looked up from her cup of tea, her eyes darkened by Alina's words.

"Yeah, the last month, every day practically, he found pleasure in that, I think. He would beat me and then he would take me. Look, I'm sorry to have to tell you this but I think you need to know."

Aisha shuddered; she couldn't imagine the Prince being like that. She said nothing, reflecting in silence and Alina continued, "Then one day, that was it, I guess he got tired of me and the two Turkish girls became his favorite playthings. Ever since then, he has left me alone, it's as if I didn't exist and nothing had ever happened." She dried a tear from her eye; the memory was obviously painful.

"I hate him, Aisha. He's a bastard," she hissed.

"Hush, hush now, don't cry." She went to sit beside her. "I'm sorry I made you talk about this, me and my silly romantic ideas. I'm just not very experienced I guess."

"It's ok, Aisha, don't worry about me. It's you I'm concerned about." They sat there for a while in silence, each reflecting on her situation.

"So why didn't you leave?" Aisha asked after a while.

"Where would I go? I have no one in the world. At least here I am well treated and plus, what makes you think we can leave? I'm not too sure about that possibility."

"Of course we can leave. We're only here for five years, aren't we?" Aisha was perplexed about the possibility that Alina had raised.

"I guess so, but who knows for sure. There are girls that come and go all the time, so I guess it would be ok if someone wanted to leave." Alina didn't want to elaborate on what she knew or thought on the subject. The girls left the conversation at that; both of them did not wish to explore it further.

The Prince's courtship of Aisha continued on relentlessly. He loved to seduce young and naïve girls like her; it was his favorite sport. Somehow, for him, in his twisted reasoning, it confirmed that he was a great conqueror of women. Every night he had her sit with him, he brought her horseback riding, on visits of the kingdom, and on his falconine trips. Although she had serious reservations about him, Aisha was thrilled; she loved the power he exuded and all the pomp. He showered her with compliments, jewelry, and expensive gifts. Every morning, 144 pink roses were delivered to her room, and the ones from the day before were removed. When they went shopping, she always came back with a dozen dresses, shoes, and everything else that he thought she should have. She was running out of room to put everything away and had to store some of her things in Alina's room. The more the Prince courted her, the more Alina and Mohini got concerned. The most concerned of all though, was by far, Mr. Za. He did not like it when the Prince took too much time to court a girl. Who knows what one could say, the Prince was in love and it made him very nervous. He continued his visits to Aisha, even though he was more frightened than before.

"After all," he surmised, "why should only the Prince enjoy this unique beauty? Have I not left her pure for him? Anyway, he will grow tired of her, he always does."

Aisha hated every second of his nightly visits, but once he was gone, she erased it from her mind, otherwise she would go insane, she thought. Better to act as though it did not exist. Mostly, though, she was terrified that something might happen to her mother and sisters, so she suffered in silence and lived hoping that they were well.

"If you speak of this to the Prince, your whole family will die, I promise." Every time, he made the same threat to her. He would hold her hard by the arm, his crooked eye close to hers and his foul breath would fill her nostrils.

"Dead, I've given my orders, if anything happens to me because of your big mouth, they are dead, I swear on Allah's name."

"You're hurting my arm, Mr. Za, please." He released her arm and she rubbed it.

"I will keep silent, as I have always done, but please, I beg you, I would like so much to have news of my mother and sisters, please Mr. Za, ask Mr. Chen to hurry, please."

"Ok, I'll see what I can do, just remember my warning." With those words, he would leave.

Aisha went to the bathroom to cry and vomit. "God, I hate that man. I wish you to die, I hope you burn in hell for eternity, you foul, evil man." She would repeat this to herself with clenched fists, as tears poured down her cheeks. It was the first time in her life that she wished someone would die.

Meanwhile, Alina had been keeping very busy at opening Aisha's eyes about the Prince. She had forced Aisha to talk to at least ten girls; all confirmed to her that the Prince was a violent brute who treated women like cattle, mere possessions, which were interchangeable at his will. They even had tea with Gila and Fatma, the two Turkish girls. All told Aisha of orgies, with many girls participating. They also met his current amusements, as Alina liked to say, Jamila from Yemen and Parveen from Pakistan, both girls who slept with him on and off. Aisha was in a state of shock; her romantic illusions shattered. The more she heard about the Prince, the more she loathed and feared him. At the same time, she was mystified by his attitude towards her. He never made any advances, he would kiss her hand and bow to bid her good night; he was a perfect gentleman. His attitude was inconsistent with the stories she heard. So, she played along with him, the illusion that it would work out as she dreamed between them still alive, somewhere in the back of her mind.

The Prince, on the other hand, was growing tired of playing gentleman. After all these months, he was getting anxious to claim his prize and to consume it.

It was a perfect day; the azure sky and endless dunes of the desert combined with the placidity of the emerald sea afar formed a sublime oneness. The Prince and Aisha were racing down the beach on two powerful black Arabian stallions, reigning them in when they came up to a large round tent that had been set up close to the sea. They dismounted quickly and servants took the foaming horses away.

"You ride well, Aisha, you are strong yet fluid with the horse. He loves to obey you. You are a natural rider." Both were sweating and a bit out of breath; although it was early morning, the day was already hot.

"Thank you, Your Highness, all I know I have learned from you. You are an excellent rider and teacher. I, on the other hand, am merely one of your good students." Aisha had learned the necessity of flattery with a person as vain as the Prince.

"Ha, ha, yes indeed, you are an excellent student, Aisha. You impress me. Come, let us go inside." The Prince motioned to her to step inside the tent. The setup inside was lavish; the floor was covered with fine rugs, on which had been laid out an array of cushions large and small. Large fans were blowing and it made the tent cool. The cool air felt good on the two riders' skin, in contrast to the heat outside. Several servants were scurrying about, bringing food and refreshments and setting them about. Aisha and the Prince went to the center of the room where the Prince's place had been set. They took off their white linen robes, which they always wore to ride.

"May I?" Aisha pointed to her veil.

"Yes, please do." The Prince looked at her tenderly as she revealed her face. "You are more than beautiful you know."

"How is that, Your Highness?"

"Because your beauty is rare as a precious stone, brighter than any star, warmer than the sun, and has the delicacy of a butterfly in flight."

Aisha looked to the ground, feigning bashfulness. Inspired by her apparent approval he continued, "You are also strong and proud, you walk as a queen walks. The fire of life burns within you and lights up everything and everyone around you. That is why you are more beautiful than beautiful, because you are unique, none like you has existed before and none will exist after you." He smiled and motioned to her to have a seat among the cushions.

"Thank you, Your Highness; you are so kind and generous in your words to me. I feel I do not deserve so many compliments. I am really a simple girl, you know."

"Simple, maybe in your ways, yes, but highly intelligent. Haven't you learned our language in three months?" Aisha looked at him, surprised.

"Of course I know," he smiled. "I pay these people; it is their job to tell me what goes on and who makes progress and who doesn't. I also know that all our 'guests' and servants think very highly of you, that you are the queen of their hearts. As for me, I consider you an angel sent to me by the almighty, as a sign of his pleasure for my generosity"

"Thank you, Your Highness. Once again I say, you are too kind, I am flattered and lost for words as what to say after such eloquent praise." The truth of the matter was that Aisha was getting a little bored with the Prince's soliloquies. She'd heard most of them at least twice and they were starting to fall flat, plus, she just could not get out of her mind, all the things the other girls had told her about him.

"Think nothing of it, Aisha; you deserve all the praise that is showered on you." The Prince raised his tea glass to her and smiled. Aisha smiled back and took a sip of the sweet, warm tea. It was good to be in the cool tent, away from the sun. Servants arrived and placed some plates of traditional food in front of them.

"Who were all those people outside, Your Highness? They seemed to be expecting you, if I may ask, of course?" Aisha was always very careful to remain polite to the utmost.

"You may. They are desert people. The heads of each tribe shall be allowed in shortly. They are here to ask my guidance about certain problems they have. It is a tradition with my people."

"What kind of problems, Your Highness?"

"Problems with wives, daughters, marriages, or with camels or sheep, or other questions of property and sometimes there are feuds between families or tribes and there is a difference to be settled, you will see after we eat. You will have to put your veil back on though; these people are very traditional you know."

"Yes of course, Your Highness." They began to eat.

"So, tell me, what else have you been studying that you have not told me about?" The Prince's tone was slightly mocking, but still polite.

"I have been reading about America a lot. It sounds like a fascinating place."

A frown came over the Prince's brow. He looked at her with fire in his eyes. "America, you say." He spoke in Arabic now. "It is the Mecca of the infidels, inhabited by corruption and vice. It shall be destroyed, eaten by the inside because of its' own viciousness and greed."

Aisha was stunned by the Prince's acerbic words, when he expressed himself in his mother tongue; she detected a very hostile edge in his voice.

"Have you been there, Your Highness?" she asked hesitantly.

"Yes I have and with my own eyes, I have seen inside the heart of the beast. I fear for the future, my angel, I fear for the future." The Prince stared at the plates, lost in his thoughts.

It was the first time that he had called her that, "my angel." It felt strange and disconcerting to hear him say that. Aisha decided not to press the issue further. She had seen something sinister in the Prince's eyes, something dark and angry, which was deep and potentially violent; it frightened her. Her professor, Mr. Rowling, a British diplomat, who was also the Prince's bridge partner, would certainly not have agreed with him about America, he had told her wonderful things about America and Europe.

"It is the land of the free," he had said. "All have a chance to make it on their own, there is work for the willing, all go to school and no one goes hungry."

"Someday I shall go there and send for my mother and sisters," she had told him.

The Prince broke into her thoughts, the cloud of his outburst dissipated. "Tonight, I have prepared a great feast for you, my precious one. There will be decorations, fireworks, entertainment, food and drinks, all in your honor."

"But Your Highness, it is not my birthday, so why a feast in my honor?"

"Because I have a surprise for you, my precious and pretty one, and yes, it is your birthday in a way, but, let us not spoil the surprise." He did not elaborate further and turned to a guard nearby, gave him an order and he signaled to Aisha to put her veil back on.

A group of twenty tribesmen came in the tent. All bowed deeply to the Prince and sat on the rug with their legs crossed, directly in front of Aisha and the Prince. The servants offered them tea and food. As the Prince had said, they all had some advice or permission to ask. Mostly it was about women or sheep or camels. "My third wife is being difficult with me. She has given me three sons, but now she has become cold and indifferent to me. I give her gifts and am a good husband, nothing changes, what can I do?"

Another had a dispute about camels with another tribesman; yet another wanted to marry his fourteen-year-old daughter to a sixty-two-year-old man and wanted the Prince's permission. The consultation went on for over four hours. Aisha listened intently; these people fascinated her. They were from another era. The Prince listened to all with infinite politeness. He asked questions, gave his advice or permission when needed. No matter how trivial, he gave all questions equal consideration. This ancient tribal tradition was obviously very important to him. When it was over, they mounted fresh horses and rode back to the palace. Aisha loved to ride the Prince's thoroughbreds, dashing madly along the beach at a furious pace. The horses knew they were going home and always went faster on the way back.

That evening, as promised by the Prince, there was a huge feast in Aisha's honor. It was an incredible party; the Prince had left nothing out. Elegant tents had been set out in a large circular formation on the grounds. Every type of food was available; there were acrobats, flamethrowers, jugglers, musicians, and snake charmers. The whole area was decorated with multicolored balloons and ribbons. All the girls were there, dressed up and excitedly chatting and eating in small groups. The girls always loved a party, no matter what the reason was. In this case, none of them really knew what the occasion was and none of them cared. The Prince and Aisha were on a special podium that had been set up to overlook the scene. The area was lit by hundreds of oil lanterns perched on wooden poles. Servants were everywhere bustling about their business and a full moon lit the sky above them. To an outsider, the scene would have appeared surreal, incarnating the opulence and the excesses that were inherent to the palace, a historical anachronism, a living reminder of ancient times, when power was omnipotent and absolute, and people were mere pawns that rulers used, elevated or eliminated, at their whim.

The Prince was happy. It was a successful feast and he contemplated Aisha from the corner of his eyes. She was serene, poised, smiling to her friends, and oblivious to his gaze. The Prince raised his arm, it was a signal, fireworks lit up the sky; there were "ohs'" and "ahs'" all around. Aisha looked up at the exploding sky and thought of her mother and sisters.

"God I wish they were here with me, to see this magnificence, this beauty. I miss them so much." The Prince interrupted her in her train of thought.

He reached over and took her hand in his. She became rigid; it was the first time that he had touched her in that way.

"So, my precious, are you enjoying the evening?" He did not release her hand.

She turned to look at him. "Yes, Your Highness, I am lost with words to express my joy and gratitude." She looked up at the fireworks. "It's magnificent, thank you, Your Highness, thank you so very much."

The Prince smiled at her; he stroked her hand with his other free hand. A slight tremor traveled down Aisha's spine. She apprehended what these gestures might be announcing.

"Now, my precious angel, I have a little surprise for you." He pulled something from under his robe, a small red velvet box. He opened it and pulled out a fine platinum necklace adorned by a river of diamonds. He held it up. The beauty of the jewelry impressed Aisha.

"Here, allow me, precious." The Prince let go of her hand and motioned to her to turn around. He put the necklace around her neck and she turned to face him. He lifted his hand, and a servant came with a mirror and placed it in front of her. Aisha touched it; it was sublime, scintillating in the evening light.

"Your Highness, it is so beautiful, I do not deserve this, it is too much, I…"

"Hush, my precious, hush now." He took her hand again. "It is normal that you receive such a gift, for tonight is a very special night. Tonight you will become a woman and I wanted you to remember this night as a very special evening."

Aisha felt like she had been punched in the stomach, but she remained composed. She knew this was coming, she had prepared for it, she was ready, she only wished it had come later, or never at all.

"But Your Highness, I am already a woman," she feigned not to understand his words, looking him innocently into the eyes.

"Yes my precious, you are," his gaze boring into hers, "but tonight you will be my woman." Their eyes remained locked for a long time, each unwavering. Aisha turned her head away first and she looked up to the fireworks.

"They're so pretty; it makes the sky even more beautiful than it is already. Don't you agree, Your Highness?"

The Prince looked up, without letting go of her hand. "Yes, my precious, they are magnificent." Aisha did not dare look anywhere else; she was afraid her growing anxiety would become apparent to him.

Once the fireworks were over, the Prince rose and he helped Aisha stand up. "Come, my precious, let us go."

He led her down the stairs. Guards and servants followed along as they made their way through the crowd of girls. Aisha's heart was pounding furiously; the faces of the girls were one big blur to her. They walked in silence towards the Prince's quarters in the main building and soon they were standing in the middle of his immense chambers.

"Come, Aisha, let me show you around." He took her hand and they walked around the place. It was unimaginably luxurious, there were gold fixtures on all the baths, hundreds and hundreds of clothes and shoes in multiple walk-ins, French antiques, Italian paintings, Chinese vases, and an array of just about everything expensive or ostentatious imaginable. The combination of which, was a *nouveau riche tableau,* of incredible bad taste. There was a terrace large enough to hold a hundred people, with a breathtaking view of the grounds and the desert in the distance. Of course the *piece de resistance* was the bed. It was enormous and large enough for a whole family to sleep in comfortably. It was adorned with elegant multicolored cushions covered in the richest of silks and had a remote control that the Prince showed Aisha could make the bed go in any direction. The Prince brought her to one of the three living rooms of the chambers. He had ordered tea and biscuits for them. The room was illuminated by the light of hundreds of candles, as were all the rooms of the chambers. Arabian music played in the background and the odor of incense filled the air. The Prince stood in front of Aisha and he gently passed his hand in her hair and touched her cheek. Tears began to pour down her face uncontrollably,

"What is it, my precious? What is wrong? Come, sit over here." He had her sit in a large, oversized couch covered in gaudy red velvet. Aisha was trembling from head to feet. The Prince gave her a handkerchief and sat beside her.

"Come now, no need to cry, tell me what is troubling you, my precious? I am your Prince, I can help. Is it I? Do I frighten you so that you tremble like a palm branch in the wind?" He took her hand and stroked it gently.

"No, Your Highness, it is not you. You have been most kind and generous to me. It's just that I'm not ready for this, you know, to be a woman. I'm just not ready, that's all." Aisha bowed her head, still sniffling.

"It's ok, my angel, my precious, there is no hurry, your Prince is a Prince after all and he may do as he wishes. So we shall wait for you to be ready. There is time, everything will be all right, you will see." He took Aisha by the shoulders and pulled her towards him, pressing her against his chest. The smell of his manhood and his cologne entered her nostrils. The former reminded her of Mr. Za and it repulsed her. The Prince still held her and was passing one of his hands on her shoulders in a comforting way, at the same time he was gently rocking her, as one would rock a baby. Aisha had stopped crying and was a bit calmer.

"There now, my precious, my angel, that is better. Tell me, do you love your Prince? Is he not good for you?"

The question caught Aisha by surprise, she moved her head affirmatively against his chest, out of instinct; it was the only answer she could give and she knew it.

"Good and he loves you too, very much you know. You are a gift from the almighty and I shall treat you as such, do not be afraid." He finally let her go and put his hand under her chin, lifting her head,

"Let me get the guards to bring you back to your room, so you can rest. Tomorrow you will feel better. Do not worry about all this; it is normal for a man and a woman who are in love to be with each other. It is the way the almighty planned it. We have time, all will be well, you'll see. It is a very enjoyable experience and you'll like it, I promise. Now come, just go and relax and remember your Prince loves you as much as you love him."

Aisha could not speak, as she was a bit dumfounded by his declaration of love. She acquiesced with her head that she understood. The Prince took it to mean that she loved him. Then again, he was sure that any woman in the world would fall in love with him if he had a bit of time with her. He considered his charm infallible. He helped Aisha get up and walked her towards the door. He ordered a guard to walk her to her room and motioned to the other one to step in.

"Good night now, my precious, sleep well."

Aisha bowed to him. "Thank you, Your Highness, good night to you too." Aisha began to walk down the corridor with the guard in tow.

When she was out of hearing range, the Prince turned to the guard standing beside him and said, "Go get me Mr. Za." The guard left precipitously to get Mr. Za.

"Yes Your Highness?" Mr. Za was out of breath. He had come as fast as he could.

"Get me Jamila, I need her now." He was obviously not in his best mood.

"What is it with the girl Aisha, Your Highness? I thought tonight was the big night, if I may ask, of course." He lowered his head in a gesture of submission.

"No you may not, Mohamed, but since you have, well, she was not feeling well so I sent her to her room. Now, if you don't have any other questions, would you do as I say?" The Prince turned and went back into his chambers. It was a signal to Mr. Za that the conversation was over.

"No Your Highness, no questions. I will get her immediately, Your Highness," he said as he left the room, walking backwards and bowing to the Prince's back.

Mr. Za chuckled as he walked towards the House of the Pure to fetch Jamila. In all these years, he had never seen the

Prince have such patience with a girl as he did with Aisha. "I think he is taken with this one," he thought, "more than he knows or wants to admit to himself, but, he will tire of this little game and she will soon learn who is in charge." He chuckled again as he scurried to attend to his urgent task.

Aisha sat on her bed and was trembling slightly. She had escaped him this time, but how long could she hold him off? Sooner or later, she knew, he would prevail, that was a certainty. The thought made her queasy. She hated how he had touched her and looked at her. She did not want to be with this man. Desperately she searched her mind for a way out, a way not to be his, not to be one of his possessions. Alina's words of the first day she had arrived at the palace now rang in her head: "This place," she had said, "this place is a prison." Just then, Aisha was startled by an all-too-familiar knock on the door.

The next day, Aisha was upset all day. Now that the Prince had made his first move, she knew that time was running out. She confided everything to Alina, who was of no real comfort. "Just go with the flow, Aisha, what else is there to do? Anyway, whatever you do, don't get him mad, trust me, you do not want to get him mad, mark my words."

"Ok, ok, I won't, thanks for nothing." She returned to her room in even worse spirits than before.

Aisha could not concentrate on her studies or think straight; she was very perturbed.

That very evening, the Prince had her sit with him, as had been the case for the last months. He was gentle, kind, and considerate. They had a good conversation and shared tea. Aisha actually laughed at a few things he said and she forgot about her emotional turmoil of the day. The Prince walked her back to her room and kissed her hand for a long time, much too long for her liking.

They played this little scenario for a few more weeks. Each time the Prince became more adventurous, touching her hair and face, kissing her forehead and telling her he loved her. Aisha did not respond; she remained stiff and tense. She would only nod her head when he asked her if she loved him too. The Prince took this reaction to be caused by her shyness and uncertainty as a woman. He was convinced that she was head over heels in love with him. Once Aisha was in her room, she would let out an immense sigh of relief. Her hope was that his passion would die, or somehow go away. It did not.

Then one night, at about two A.M., there was a knock on her door. Aisha got out of bed. She was sure it was Mr. Za, "that bloody pervert, at this hour." She opened the door briskly. It was he. She eyed him with disdain and defiance.

He did not attempt to come in. "The master wishes to see you," he said in his official tone.

"What, now?"

"Yes, now."

Aisha was surprised, but she knew there was no discussion.

"Very well, give me ten minutes, I shall be ready." She closed the door in his face, which gave her a small amount of pleasure.

She followed Mr. Za in silence along the darkened corridors. They reached the Prince's chambers, and a guard let her in. The immense room was lit with a sea of candles. The Prince stood in a corner; he was bare-chested and had a strange look on his face. He came up to her slowly. His chest was covered with thick, black, body hair. He touched her face. He emanated a strong musky odor, mixed with alcohol. As a reflex, she turned her head from his hand. He took her face in his hand and had her look at him. They were inches apart, and she could feel the Prince's strength from the pressure his fingers exerted on her face.

"Oh my precious, you are so exquisite, so divine, you are the true work of the almighty himself." He pulled her to him and kissed her on the lips. His tongue darted in and out of her mouth. Aisha remained motionless, eyes open, she looked at him in shock. The Prince let her go and took a step back. His eyes had changed color; they were darker and more menacing.

"What is the matter with you, girl? Do you despise me? Do I smell bad? What is wrong with you?" He was pacing about, getting more agitated and angry by the second. His voice was loud and aggressive. This was the Prince that Aisha had been warned about. She stared to the ground, too terrified to speak or look at him.

"Answer me!" he shouted to her face. He took her by the shoulders and shook her violently. "Do you hate me? Speak I say."

"No, I do not hate you, I...."

The Prince shook her again, oblivious to what she was saying. The rage and the alcohol had pushed him over the brink. "Then why do you not act as a woman should with me? You are like a lifeless piece of dead meat." He shook her again and pushed her back. He circled around her. "Speak I say, speak now." His tone was threatening and ominous.

"Your Highness, it's just that..." Aisha could not finish her sentence. She began to sob and put her hands to her face. His anger was just too much for her.

The sight of her crying drove him to madness. He screamed louder. "Is that all you're good for? Crying like a baby? What's wrong with you, you're a woman, look!" With those words he ripped the robe from her body and threw it in a corner. Aisha stood there trembling in her bra and underwear. The Prince took a step back, silenced for a moment by her exquisite beauty so revealed. He grabbed her arm and dragged her to the bed. He threw her on it, ripping off her bra and panties with swift powerful movements. He jumped on the bed and ravished her violently. Even though the pain was excruciating, Aisha did not utter a sound, submitting to his savage thrusts over and over again. The assault went on for hours and every time he had an orgasm, he would grunt like a wild animal. After a few hours, he was finally spent. He rolled over and fell asleep. Aisha waited. When he began to snore, she got up and silently picked up her torn clothes, put them on, and left the chambers.

For hours, she lay in her bath, staring at the wall, in a state of shock. She was sore down there, but mostly she was sore in her soul. She felt dirty, cheated and violated, to the very sanctity of her inner being. That night, like so many nights before, she cried herself to sleep.

It was Alina who woke her up the next morning, Aisha had overslept. Noticing her red eyes she asked, "Hey, what's wrong?"

Aisha told her what had happened the night before, omitting no details.

"That fucking bastard, I told you not to get him mad. Well, at least he didn't beat you." Alina took Aisha in her arms and they both began to cry. Alina tried comforting Aisha as best she could.

"Its ok, everything will be ok, I'm here and I'll look out for you. Just hear me when I try to tell you something, I've been there Aisha, I tried to warn you."

"I know Alina, I know." The girls stayed a long time in each other's arms, crying and rocking each other gently.

They did not see the Prince for three days and then on the fourth day, the roses started arriving at Aisha's room again. The girls were informed that the Prince would be there that evening. Aisha did not know how she should act with him. Pretend that nothing had happened? How could she? He had raped her, the pig. She was angry as hell, yet she also knew that anger was not an option. She paced around her room for hours, until it was time for her to go and face him.

The Prince was his usual charming self. He acted as though nothing had happened. He had Aisha sit with him; he told her stories of his trips abroad, drank tea and was rather merry. Aisha listened politely, interjecting only when necessary and laughing lightly at his ignorant jokes. Inside, Aisha was seething; she now knew the brute that was in front of her. She looked at him and smiled while thinking, "You can have my body you animal, but you will never have my heart and soul." The thought gave her strength and courage and it made her feel superior to him.

Near the end of the evening, the Prince came closer to her. "I must speak to you of the other night." He paused. "I have felt terrible for the last three days and have been unable to sleep for as many nights. It is the alcohol; it drives me to insanity, my precious. I must not touch it, for I am become sick with it in my head." He took one of her hands and stroked it. "You must forgive me, my angel. I have prayed hard to the almighty for the past three days and nights. I have made promises to him that I intend to keep. I shall be good to you, I promise. You are like another sun, which lights up the sky and warms the earth." He motioned to the sky with his hand. Aisha said nothing; the pain in her soul was too profound. The Prince considered her silence as an acknowledgment that she forgave him. He leaned slightly back, still holding her limp hand, content with his evening and convinced that Aisha had forgiven him everything.

That night, in his chambers, he took her again many times, but she remained of stone, letting him do as he wanted with her. He hurt her with his abruptness, but it was nothing compared to the pain that inhabited her heart. Finally he was spent and he lay besides her, catching his breath.

"You do not make love to me, my angel, I make love to you. I'm sorry, I'm so sorry I have hurt you, but I will better myself, I promise. I will be good to you and teach you about love. You will see how good it can be and that you can enjoy it as much as me."

"Thank you Your Highness, that is most kind and generous of you." Aisha's tone was flat and unexpressive. The Prince didn't even notice, so certain he was of his sexual effect on women, any woman. After all, it was not the first time that a woman had resisted him. He was convinced that she would come around, as they all did eventually. Actually the majority pretended to like him and enjoy having sex with him; however, he was oblivious to that.

Aisha, however, did not come around; each night, whether he took her with force or with tenderness, she would have no reaction. Her kisses were lifeless, without passion. She never said, "I love you," as the other girls did. She would not, she could not, bring herself to pretend that she had any feelings for this brutal, insensitive man. She was of stone and the more he pressed her, the more her resolve and bitterness grew. The Prince, on the other hand, was getting more and more frustrated with her. It was not enough that he had her body to do as he wished, he wanted her soul too. He bought her gifts of all kinds, threw parties for her, brought her on trips to the desert. Nothing worked; she remained compact and cold as ice. He begged, he pleaded, he wooed and he was convinced that he was madly in love with her. The more she resisted him, the more his crooked sentiment grew. To all his sweet words and languorous poems, she would only answer, "Thank you, Your Highness, for your kindness and generosity to me. I do not deserve such praise."

She would say this while looking him straight in the eyes and adorning an angelic smile. Her haughtiness, poise, and dignity enraged him even more. He had run out of ideas to try to win her over. So he would leave the palace on trips abroad, where he would drink ferociously and was violent and obnoxious with everything and everyone. He had two or three girls a night brought to him. It was to no avail, nothing worked, he could not get Aisha out of his system. He was infected with her, her indifference ran through his veins, and it made him moody and volatile. The concoctions of these elements were the ingredients of a recipe that announced dire things to come.

One morning, Aisha was awakened by Alina; who was crying and shaking and unable to speak. Aisha sat up in her bed. "What, what is it, Alina? Tell me, are you ill? What's wrong?" It was impossible to understand what she said because of her sobbing.

Finally, after a few tries, she managed to blurt out, "Something terrible has happened, Aisha, it's horrible," she choked and was unable to continue.

Aisha took her by the shoulders and said, "Alina, breath in deeply and please tell me what happened."

"It's Jamila; we were supposed to play tennis together this morning before breakfast. So I went to get her in her room and... and...I saw..." She broke up again and pointed with her hand shaking violently in the directions of Jamila's room. Aisha got out of bed and quickly got dressed.

"Ok, you stay here; I'll go see what's wrong."

"It's horrible, Aisha, you shouldn't go, just call the guards." Alina was terribly distraught.

"I'm going, just stay put." Aisha ignored her, walked out, and went briskly towards Jamila's room, four doors down from hers.

The door was partially opened. She pushed it open and went into the room. She was not prepared for what she saw. Jamila's body was hanging by the neck in front of her patio door. A stool had been knocked sideways below her. She had hung herself with a bed sheet that she had passed through a big iron hook that was imbedded in the exterior cement wall. Aisha walked up to the body. It was not a pretty sight to see. Jamila's face was badly bruised and cut. Her neck and shoulders were exposed and they were covered with black and blue bruises, as well as her legs. Obviously, she had been severely beaten.

The first thought that came to Aisha's mind was, "is this a suicide or is it a murder disguised as a suicide?" She looked around the room and that's when she saw it. A letter had been placed on the desk. She walked over and took it in her hands. It was sealed and addressed to Jamila's parents. Aisha put it down the front of her jeans and walked out of the room. She saw a guard down the hall and walked up to him. He stared at the floor when she stood directly in front of him.

"Get me Mr. Za, now, quickly, something bad has happened." The guard took off down the hall without having uttered a word or looking at her.

Mr. Za arrived shortly. He entered Aisha's room without knocking. "What is it this time? Have you displeased the master again?"

Aisha was sitting on her bed with an arm around the sobbing Alina. She looked up at Mr. Za, defiant, eyes filled with all the loathing she felt for him.

"Well, what is it, girl? Speak."

"It's Jamila, I think you should go look in her room," Aisha said matter-of-factly, adding nothing else. Mr. Za looked at her perplexed; he turned and went off to see what she was talking about.

Aisha turned to Alina. "Hey, what do you say we go get some coffee or something?"

"I don't feel like it, Aisha. I feel so bad about poor Jamila; did you see her?"

"Yes, I saw her. It's awful, but enough of this. Let's go, I won't take no for an answer."

"He did it Aisha, that fucking animal did it, he killed her, I'm sure of it," she hissed.

"Who did it, Alina?"

"The Prince, who else?"

"Shhh, don't say that, Alina. Keep that thought for yourself, ok?" Alina nodded her head that she understood. "Ok, come on, let's go," Aisha took her hand and helped her get up.

"Just give me a second, will you?" Aisha went to her closet and quickly took out Jamila's letter from her jeans and hid it under some sweaters. She turned and went to rejoin Alina.

As they passed in front of Jamila's room, they saw that there was a flurry of activity inside. The door was partially open and there were three guards standing in front of it. They heard Mr. Za's agitated voice coming from the room.

Later that day, Mr. Za came to see Aisha at the library.

"I must speak to you now, come with me." It was an order, not an invitation. She followed him down the hallway to a sitting area. They sat facing each other on large white sofas. Mr. Za questioned her about what had happened that morning, what she had seen, at what time she had entered the room, had she spoken to anybody about it, and so on. Aisha answered all his questions, omitting to mention the letter she had found and the fact that she knew Jamila had been beaten, probably to near death. She told him only what she knew he wanted to hear.

"All I saw was her body hanging there, Mr. Za. It's so terrible that she should commit suicide like that. As for anyone else being involved, well, Alina is the only other person that I have spoken to about this, sir, but then again, she saw Jamila's body before I did."

"Very well then, now listen to me very carefully. You will speak to no one about this, no one, do you understand?"

"Yes, Mr. Za, I do." Aisha knew that tone too well; Mr. Za meant business.

"Good, I will also warn your little foul-mouthed Russian friend. I am sure she will be as understanding as you are. Now, here is the story you must remember. We will tell everyone that Jamila has gone home because of a family emergency. Her grandmother was very ill and she had been sent for. Do you follow me so far?" Aisha nodded her head. "I will be very displeased if anyone started spreading a different story about Jamila's sudden departure. The Prince and the royal family would also be very displeased." Mr. Za stared at her intently. The skin on his face was oily and sweaty; he was obviously stressed out.

"I will be silent, Mr. Za. I will do as you say."

Mr. Za smiled, happy with her submissiveness. "Fine, you may return to your studies now, we are finished talking." Aisha rose without another word and headed back to the library. Mr. Za watched her walk away.

"Such a fine woman," he thought, "but the Prince is so childish about this one. After all, she is just a woman. Women must obey their man, it is so simple, horses are made for us to ride, sheep to feed and clothe us, and women to give us pleasure and children. It is the will of the almighty. I do not understand that the master does not understand this and bring his will to bear with this woman." Maybe the rumors were founded, and the Prince's mind was troubled, as he had overheard members of the royal family say. Mr. Za sat there a long time reflecting on these profound considerations which troubled him so. "Ah the modern world," he concluded, "it is so hard to understand." With that he rose and went to look for Alina.

Aisha went back to the library, the words of Mr. Za still ringing in her ear. It made her wonder about every time a girl had left the House of the Pure in the past. It always happened mysteriously and quickly. They were always told after the girl had gone; there were never any good-byes or farewell parties. The girls never wrote and they were never heard of again. Now, she wondered where they really went. Staring at her book, lost in her thoughts, for the first time in her life she was scared, really scared. She opened her book and retrieved the letter she had taken from Jamila's room that morning. She looked around to make sure no one was looking. The letter was still unopened. She flipped it over and caressed it; slowly she opened it, delicately so as not to rip the envelope or its contents. It was a three-page letter written in Arabic. It had obviously been hastily written. There were smudges of blood on two of the pages. She read the letter slowly; her command of written Arabic was not very good. It was addressed to Jamila's parents. She told them how much she loved them and all her brothers and sisters. She said that she regretted deeply what she was about to do, but her life here had become unlivable for her. She went on to tell everything about the Prince and what went on in the palace. How he had forced her to do the worst sexual things, to be with other women, how he took her in unnatural ways and so on. She told them of the beatings; all severe and for no apparent reasons. She concluded by saying that he was a savage brute who kept fifty women here at any given time and that some were treated even worse than she was. The last paragraph was heartbreaking:

Tonight was the worst it has ever been beloved parents. I am beaten all over and my body and soul ache and hurt terrible. I have decided to take away my body from the devil's power and confine my soul to the care of the almighty. I love you all and will see you in heaven.

Your loving daughter

Jamila

The last page was smudged with blood and tears and Aisha quickly folded the letter and hid it in her book. She wiped a tear from her face and for a long time she sat wondering how she had ended up in this horrible place, at the mercy of these men who were capable of the worst and then some. Mostly though, she wondered if she would ever get out of the palace alive.

That evening, Aisha decided she would write her story from beginning to end. Where she came from, her family, Mr. Chen, and how she ended up in the palace. She would describe the place and its inhabitants, but mostly she would chronicle what went on here in very minute detail. She took a black hardcover notebook that she had not used for school. She placed Jamila's letter in the middle and she began to write. "My name is Aisha Sayuno, I am nineteen years old, and I have been living in the palace of Prince Abdul Khalid Mohamed Al-Turki for nearly two years. I live in a section of the palace called the House of the Pure, which is exclusively reserved for the Prince's women. We are about fifty at any given time. I was born in the Philippines; my family was extremely poor and…"

So, every night from then on, Aisha wrote her story. She was very meticulous and left out no details or names. She had found an excellent hiding place for the notebook, jammed into the underbelly of one of her sofas. No one could find it, even inadvertently. God forbid it should fall in the hands of Mr. Za and she shuddered at the idea. Her hope was that if she did not get out of the palace alive, her notebook would get out and tell her story. The Prince's abusive lifestyle would then be known to the whole world, and he would be exposed. These thoughts and her writing were what kept her from losing her mind completely.

After Jamila's death, the Prince became more moody and violent than before with her. He would summon Aisha to his chambers at different hours of the day or night. He was often intoxicated with drugs or alcohol or both. He was a far cry from the charming romantic that he had portrayed himself to be. He took her violently and repeatedly; he was insatiable. He spoke little during those bouts, contenting himself of grunting, or shouting at her mockingly, "Ah, so you love me now, precious? Tell your Prince how much you love him, tell him."

"Yes, I love you."

"Louder I can't hear you."

"I love you, I love you, I love you," Aisha repeated the phrase to match every one of his thrusts. The words pronounced by her, for some strange reason made him have an orgasm. She only had to put as much sincerity as possible when she said it, but then again, by now, she had become an excellent actress.

It was a lesson she had learned the hard way. One night, she had not answered his question and he had slapped her hard in the face and punched her in the stomach. He had gotten off her, as her non-response had made him lose his erection. She was bent over in pain and bleeding from the mouth.

"Get out of here," he had yelled, "Get out now." He had grabbed her by the hair and thrown her out of the room naked, throwing her clothes at her. She had dressed in the corridor, shaking and bleeding. The two guards nearby never moved; they just stared at the floor.

The next day, she looked at her bruised face in dismay, hoping that things would get better. They did not. The beatings got worse; he would hit her for no reason, no matter how submissive she was. His outbursts were sudden and unprovoked. The Prince knew deep down in his soul that she did not love him and that she probably hated his guts. This realization drove him to punish her, the only way he knew how, with his fists. He swore to himself that he would break her will, even if he had to kill her; he had broken others before. But his behavior only made Aisha tougher and even more turned into herself. She had built a sanctuary inside her soul that was impenetrable and unattainable by him. The more he abused her, the more defiant and determined she became. "You will not have me, you animal," she told herself over and over.

The situation was becoming increasingly volatile and dangerous. Mr. Za was very concerned; he tried to get the Prince interested in some new girls that had just arrived. It was to no avail; he was obsessed with Aisha. Her presence in his palace drove him to excesses and to the brink of sanity. He was violent with all and would break objects in fits of rage. Her pain was the only thing that made him feel better. "She will hurt as I hurt," he would say out loud, as he paced aimlessly about his chambers. "She will suffer with me and by me, until she gives me her heart. I want all of her," he would yell at Mr. Za, in one of his intoxicated rages. "Get me her heart, Mohamed, it is an order." Mr. Za got more and more worried as the Prince's state of mind deteriorated. He pleaded with Aisha, he threatened and was convinced, that should the Prince continue on this slippery course, his own life was at stake. After one such volatile session with the Prince, he stormed into Aisha's room.

"But Mr. Za," she pleaded, "I do everything he wants, when he wants, I don't know what else I can do." Aisha was afraid of Mr. Za; she knew what kind of a man he could be. She did not like to see him this way. Mr. Za paced about the room nervously.

"I don't know, girl, do something. I have never seen His Highness this way. Stop being so hard-headed, you will destroy us all." He was very agitated, his eyes bulging out of their sockets, beads of sweat forming on the side of his head.

"I am not hard-headed, I swear Mr. Za, I am obedient and my only wish is to make His Highness happy. I want to please him, but the more I try, the angrier he seems to get."

"But don't you see, girl, the Prince is like a child." His tone became softer and pleading. "He needs to be caressed and loved; you have to make him feel that he has all of you. Is that so hard? Every woman knows how to do that. You must try harder, harder, do you understand?" He was standing near her face and Aisha could smell his foul breath. He grabbed her by the hand and dragged her towards the sofa. He had her get on her knees and he sat down exposing his penis. "Come now, make me forget that you are so disobedient," he said, as he pushed her head forcefully down between his legs.

The cycle of abuse continued on for weeks and months, to Aisha, it became a routine. She felt nothing and lost track of time and place. For days she lived in a stupor like state, beaten and violated by the Prince and abused by Mr. Za. There seemed to be no end to it and she became a dull, lifeless, empty being, heartbroken and disillusioned, her body broken and her soul empty and had lost all faith in human beings and life itself.

Her only salvation was her studies and she studied with a vengeance. She devoured everything she could get her hands on, be it history, literature, philosophy, and even theology. Every spare moment she had she spent reading or writing. She also kept her little black book up to date. Every new abuse, every beating was explicitly recorded. The arrival and departure of girls, their names, the dates, and what country they came from. Her friend Alina stayed away from her now that Aisha was bad news with the Prince; she did not want to be associated with her. Ever since Jamila's death, Alina was obsessed with leaving the palace and going back to Russia. She feared that her friendship with Aisha would hinder her chances of being sent home. So Aisha kept to herself. She didn't mind, though; she liked being alone, she lived in her head, blocking out all the horrible things that she lived on a daily basis. Only Mohini remained a friend and a confidant.

She knew what was going on; she would come to Aisha's room and try to comfort her and mend her bruises. Many nights, Aisha had fallen asleep after having cried her heart out in Mohini's arms.

"Poor child," she would whisper in her ear, "this man is crazy, I'm afraid for you, this has to stop child; you must speak with His Highness." Her voice was filled with anguish, Aisha knew that voice; it was the voice of her youth, the voice of the helpless and was all too familiar to her. She did not respond to what Mohini said, it had become a ritual between them; they both knew that there was nothing that could be done. The only hope was that the Prince would tire of Aisha and pass his rage on someone else. So, Mohini would take care of her as best she could, especially the two or three days that she had to stay in her room after a severe beating. Mr. Za did not allow her to go out of her room if she was bruised. Those few days were good times for Aisha. She had someone who loved her and took care of her and it was a soothing balm, on her otherwise brutal existence.

But the Prince's rage did not subside, it got worse. It was as if something had broken in his primitive mind. Aisha had unwittingly set off something which brought out the worst in him and she and Mr. Za now had something very real in common; they both feared for their lives.

It was in this environment that Mr. Chen showed up again. He had been summoned by Mr. Za, who hoped that he could help him with Aisha. He was convinced that she was making the Prince go insane and he had asked Mr. Chen to stay as long as it took to try to solve the problem. Mr. Za set him up in a room that was a few doors down from his own. Although Mr. Za was sincere in trying to make him comfortable, Mr. Chen was not happy to spend any amount of time at the palace in close quarters with Mr. Za. It was not his definition of an interesting time and he was irritated at the perspective and was in a foul mood.

"You will stay the time it takes, the situation is very serious," Mr. Za's had told him, it had been more an order than a plea. Mr. Chen had nodded and agreed in silence. The Prince was his most important customer and he knew that he would have to do whatever it took to remedy the situation.

Aisha was summoned to Mr. Za's room, where a guard let her in. Mr. Za was sitting at a small desk, writing; he did not look up when she came in. She walked up to the front of the desk.

"You have asked for me?" She looked around; she had never been in Mr. Za's room before. There was a single bed in a corner and very little furniture. The room was smaller than her own and very Spartan.

"Yes." He rose. "There is a visitor here to see you." Aisha's eyes brightened,

"Is it Mr. Chen? Tell me please, is it Mr. Chen? Has he brought news of my family?" Aisha was excited.

"Yes, it is Mr. Chen, calm down now, come and follow me." He led her out of his room and down the corridor to Mr. Chen's room. He knocked on the door, Mr. Chen opened up.

"Come in." He stepped aside, Aisha walked in, and Mr. Chen closed the door behind her. Mr. Za did not follow her in.

"Sit down." Mr. Chen motioned to a chair in the corner.

Ignoring the command, Aisha turned to him and said, "I want news of my mother and sisters." She was surprised by the harshness of her own voice. "I have not heard from them for more than a year. How come my mother does not answer my letters? What has happened? I want to know."

"Silence!" he shouted. Aisha was stunned by his shout, and sat down. "How dare you speak to me like that, girl? Who do you think you are? You have been very bad and only trouble for me!" He was shouting and pacing around the room; he was angry, very angry. "Your stupid mother was involved in some serious trouble. She was caught stealing clothes at the factory. It cost me a lot of money to prevent her from going to jail. She has lost her job and her only income is the money I give her every month. The money the Prince gives me to further your education. You ungrateful little bitch."

"That's impossible, Mr. Chen. My mother would never do anything like that, I swear." Aisha was suddenly inundated with fear.

"Are you calling me a liar too now?" He came close to her, his face red with rage.

"No, Mr. Chen, of course not, sir," Aisha stared at the floor while he resumed pacing around her.

"I hear from Mr. Za that you have made the Prince very unhappy, that he has grown sullen and moody, that you have driven him to excesses because of your impoliteness to him. I will stop giving your family money, what do you have to say about that? Would you like that?" Mr. Chen was screaming now. "How dare you insult the Prince in his house, you little bitch? He who feeds and clothes you and your family, you whore, you nothing!" His anger and the horrible words he used had silenced and shocked Aisha. It was clear to her that he was a dangerous man, violent and unpredictable like the Prince. Mr. Chen's rage was not yet abated.

"You," he pointed his manicured finger at her face, "you and all your family are finished. Do you understand? Do you hear me, you little ungrateful slut? I shall have your mother and sisters murdered and thrown to the dogs." He was inches away from her face. Tears poured down her cheeks.

"No, please, Mr. Chen, I have not been bad. I have done everything I was told to do, I promise. I have done nothing wrong." Aisha fell to her knees, imploring him. "Please, Mr. Chen, please do not harm them, I will do anything, I beg you." He paced around her prostrate and sobbing body.

"You have dishonored me, girl, you have made a fool out of me. The Prince will never trust me again. All because of you, you who I have tried to help, you and your stupid family, dead I say, dead all of them"

"No, Mr. Chen, kill me instead, leave them alone, take my life, I don't care, just leave them alone." Aisha was nearly hysterical.

"I wish I could kill you, you whore, you bitch, I wish I could, but the Prince won't allow it. Even though that's all you deserve, no, your family will pay for your wickedness, someone has to pay and it will not be me."

Aisha flew across the room and threw herself at his feet, holding onto one of his legs as if her life depended on it.

"No, no, no!" she screamed. He grabbed her by the hair and lifted her to her feet, his face nearly touching hers.

"Then you had better make the Prince happy very soon, cause I will stay and make sure you do just that, or else." They were eyeball to eyeball. Aisha dared not breathe, even though his grasp on her hair hurt her.

Keeping a firm grasp on her hair, he dragged her across the room to a sofa and pushed her into a kneeling position, face down into the sofa. Kneeling behind her and still holding her firmly by the hair, he lifted her dress and with his other hand he ripped off her panties.

"I will teach you who is in command here, you little whore. From now on, you will obey, you bitch." He undid his pants. Aisha buried her head into the cushion, biting into the fabric; she knew what was coming. It was, however, much worse than she expected. With a sudden thrust, he took her in an unnatural way. She screamed into the cushion. The pain was excruciating. He was quickly done. He got up and pulled up his pants. Aisha remained face down on the cushion, sobbing and shaking. The suddenness and savagery of his attack had left her in shock.

"Get out of here now, you slut. I had better hear good things from now on, or you will get the same of this every day. I will be your teacher from here on. I will show you how things work. Now get out I say, now!" he shouted, kicking her in the shins.

Aisha lifted her head slowly from the cushion. She got up. Her panties were dangling from her ankle. With a trembling hand, she took them off and bundled them up in her hand. Without looking at Mr. Chen, she walked slowly towards the door, still shaking, and made her way back to the House of the Pure.

She stayed in her room the rest of that day, crying relentlessly. The violent and unnatural way Mr. Chen had raped her had sent a shockwave through her whole being. This was the man who had sent her here, now she understood the fear in her mother's eyes when she had left with him. "Poor Mama, did he make you suffer too? Oh, I hope not." Then again, maybe they were all dead already; that thought terrified her to the very marrow of her bones. It was more than she could bear. The assault of Mr. Chen made something snap in her mind. It sent her over the edge. The beatings of the Prince, the abuse of Mr. Za, and now Mr. Chen; it was enough, she decided, the time had come for all of it to end. A plan had been forming in her head for some time, a plan from which there was no coming back and now she would put that plan in action.

Two days later, she asked Mr. Rowling, her history teacher, to have tea with her, after one of her semiweekly courses. Aisha knew she could trust Mr. Rowling. He was a wise old diplomat, inhabited by a razor-sharp British humor, and was the epitome of politeness and civility.

"Well, Miss Aisha, what is so important that you wish to have tea in private with this old, tired man?" He sat down with the elegance and poise of his breeding and training. A servant came and poured them some tea. They were sitting at a table tucked in a corner of the library, far away from any ears or eyes, as Aisha had planned.

Aisha was nervous, but there was no going back; her decisions were made.

"First of all, you are neither old nor tired," she pretended to scold him. He smiled. "Now, Mr. Rowling," she continued, "You know how much I respect and admire your opinions and skills." Aisha paused and took a sip of her tea. Rowling said nothing; his years in the diplomatic world had taught him that flattery always precedes a request. He remained of stone, ready for anything.

"Well, as you know, I admire the English language very much and to tell you the truth. I have been secretly writing a story that I have now completed." Rowling smiled; he took a sip of his tea, knowing it would be an easy request. "You told me you are leaving soon to go back to England. I would like to give you my manuscript so you could forward it to some of your publisher friends you told me about." Aisha looked at him smiling, hoping he would take the bait. He already had.

"What's the story about? I would have to read it first, you know, to see if I believe it to be presentable."

"Of course, sir, it goes without saying, and to answer your question, it is a work of fiction, a love story of sorts." She lied admirably.

"Of course, how silly of me to ask, what other subject is there? Well, it will be my pleasure to help you in this matter Miss Aisha." He smiled content to be able to do this small favor for her.

"Thank you sir, I appreciate it. There is one very important thing however, sir."

"Yes?"

"I very much want you to read my work. As you know, your opinion is of the highest importance to me. However, I would ask you not to do so until you are home."

"But I don't leave for another two weeks, you know. Don't you wish that I read it and give you some feedback?"

"No, I insist, if I give you my manuscript, you must promise not to read it until you are home. You see, sir, if you don't like it, at least we will not have to discuss it in person, which would embarrass me terribly."

"Ok, fine, I accept your condition. I will not look at your work until I'm home, I promise."

"Thank you, sir, that is most kind and generous of you and I appreciate your generosity greatly."

Rowling scoffed, "Oh come now girl, it's nothing and a great pleasure to be of service to you."

Aisha pulled out a carefully wrapped package from her schoolbag. Inside was her black notebook. She handed it to Rowling and her hand had a slight tremor.

"There is one other little thing, Mr. Rowling."

He took the package and put it in his briefcase. "What might that be, Miss Aisha?"

"Please do not tell the Prince about this, or Mr. Za. They find I am too interested in education and the arts, you know, for a woman," she mimicked a frown.

"But of course, Aisha, do not fret; this shall be our little secret, between you and I." He winked to signal his complicity.

"Thank you, Mr. Rowling. I knew I could trust you. You are most kind, sir."

Rowling patted her hand. "Now, now, child, do not get all emotional on me, it is nothing, a small favor from one lover of the English language to another. I cannot wait to read it, and I promise that no matter what, I will write you to give you my comments. Ok?"

"Yes sir, thank you again."

Rowling rose. "Very well then, I must be off now. I will see you next week and remember to do your homework."

"I will, sir, I promise, thank you again, sir."

"Think nothing of it, happy to be of service. Good day now." Rowling tipped his large white hat and trotted off.

Aisha was relieved but scared. She gathered her things and headed quickly for her room. Once inside, she locked the door, sat down on the edge of the bed, and went through her plan again and again. She felt strongly about it and yet she was consumed by fear, and at the same time, she was inhabited by the certainty of its justness. These conflicting emotions were devouring her and she knew that only action could appease them.

She went to the hiding place where she had hidden the knife she had stolen from the kitchen. She took it in her hands; it felt good to hold it. It incarnated a strength that was beyond her body and beyond her hand. She could see her reflection in its long stainless steel blade. She caressed it slowly, turning it around, comprehending for the first time the readiness of its' sturdy seven-inch blade. She put the knife back in its hiding place and sat motionless on the edge of her bed, staring outside for the rest of the afternoon.

At six, she started to get ready. She put on a long, ample black evening dress; it was of a light black velvet and strapless. The Prince had bought it for her such a very long time ago it seemed. She did her hair and makeup and covered her shoulders with a fine matching black shawl. She looked at herself in the mirror; she was serene, poised, and looking her best. No one could have guessed that strapped on the inside of her thigh was a seven-inch stainless steel kitchen knife.

At seven, she left her room, mingling with the other girls as they headed towards the Prince's parlor. Mr. Za motioned to her when she came up to the parlor doors. He leaned over and said in her ear, "He has asked for you tonight, do not let me down." He squeezed her forearm as he spoke.

"I won't, Mr. Za, I promise. I will be good for His Highness tonight, good as never before, you will see." She smiled to him with all the false sincerity she could muster.

"Good, very good, girl, now that's the right attitude. Now go, get on with it." He pushed her slightly forward and Aisha went into the parlor.

When she sat with the Prince, she noticed that he had been drinking. She did not pick up on his sarcasm or his foul mood. She acted joyous and happy, laughing at his idiocies and feigning interest in his stories and his poetry.

"You are in a good mood tonight, my precious. This makes my heart smile. Tell me, what makes you so happy?"

"Well, you see, Your Highness, I have thought a lot lately. I have been most unkind to you and you have been most generous to me. I wish to make amends and tonight I intend to show you all my gratitude." She took his hand and kissed it, her eyes filled with the love that he had wanted to see in them for so long. He looked at her, his eyes glazed from his intoxication.

"Ah, my precious, my gift from the almighty, my prayers have been heard. I wish you only to be mine. There are no others who occupy my heart, only you," He leaned forward and kissed her hand.

"Come then, let us go now. I wish to be with you alone." They got up.

"These women," he motioned to the girls in the parlor, "they bore me and they are so common compared to you, my precious. You are the light of day; the light of my universe, to set one's eyes on you is to see the work of the almighty. Come, please." He led her down the steps and through the crowd of girls towards his private chambers. They were silent as they walked down the corridors of the palace, the silence that precedes something that must and will be.

Once in the Prince's chambers, Aisha excused herself and went to the bathroom. She unstrapped the knife and waited a few minutes. Then she very slowly opened the door of the bathroom about a quarter inch. The Prince was in the far corner, away from the bed, sitting in front of a small table, his back to her. He had taken his shirt off and was leaning forward towards the table, preparing to take drugs of some kind, as was his habit. Swiftly and silently, Aisha darted across the room, never losing sight of the Prince's back. In a rapid movement, she buried the knife under the pillows at the head of the bed.

"What are you doing, my precious? Come to me now," he said without turning, his voice thick from the alcohol and the drugs.

"I am here, Your Highness." Aisha came up behind him and put her hands on his shoulders.

"So you are," the Prince said without stopping what he was doing or looking up. He took a full glass of wine on the table and drank it down in one shot. "Ah, my precious, I feel strong tonight, I feel good. I have my Princess with me; she is mine and I am hers. Come here now, come closer to me. He took one of her hands and guided her so that she stood in front of him. His eyes were glazed over. Grabbing her by the waist, he said, "You are so beautiful, so desirable, I wish to have you now, my love." He pulled her to him, so that she sat on his legs. "Kiss me." Without waiting for a response, the Prince kissed her, his alcohol-laden tongue darting in and out of her mouth clumsily, his arm hurting the small of her back from too much pressure. Aisha played along, returning his inelegant kiss and smiling when they were done.

"Let us go lie down, Your Highness. I wish to make you happy." She took his hand, and he let himself be led to the bed, slightly off balance.

"Yes, my precious, let us lie down and be one, united as the sand is to the desert. I wish to love you now as only a man can love a woman." He let himself fall on the bed, pulling her down on top of him, his head only inches from the hidden knife. Aisha leaned towards him and kissed him passionately while slowly slipping her hand under the pillows, grabbing the knife firmly, she lifted her head slightly from the embrace, looking into the Prince's eyes. They were inches apart.

"My precious, you are so good when you want to, why have you tortured me for so long?"

Without losing his gaze, she answered. "Because you are a brute and a pig, Your Highness, and I despise you from your insides to the very extremities of your body."

The Prince's eyes became dark and perplexed and then quickly rage set in. He grabbed her by the hair and pulled her face to his. "You need a lesson woman, your head is harder than stone. I will teach you." With those words, his other hand flew and smacked her hard across the face. Aisha's head snapped back from the blow and at the same time, her hand came out from under the pillow and with a swift and powerful countermovement, she plunged the knife into the Prince's heart. He did not utter a sound; the hand that held her hair fell to his side and he looked at her in shock and disbelief. Aisha removed the knife with both hands and struck him over and over again. He had become motionless and blood was oozing from his chest, his mouth was wide open and his eyes fixed the ceiling. Aisha stared at him for a few moments, realizing that he was dead.

"Now hit me again, you rotten bastard," she shouted to the corpse. She removed the knife from his chest and then methodically cut it open, succeeding in chopping out his heart from between his ribs. She took the organ in her hands and inspected it,

"Well at least now I know you had one, Your Highness." She pried open the Prince's mouth and stuffed his heart into it. She looked at the spectacle, smiling.

"May I get something for Your Highness, or does Your Highness prefer to just lie there a bit?" She laughed out loud, the kind of laughter that is indistinguishable between the joy of the lightheaded and the dementia of the troubled mind.

Her calm returned after a while. She looked around the room; nothing moved. Her clarity came back, and she got off the Prince's body, went to the bathroom and washed herself up and cleaned her dress and the knife. She went back to the bed and covered the body with the sheets and the bedspread. Only the Prince's head was visible, from his nose up. She closed his eyes and he seemed to be asleep. She checked the room for anything that would make her deed apparent too quickly; all appeared normal. She went to the Prince's desk and opened one of the bottom drawers. She took out a large gold jewelry box. Often she had seen the Prince go through it to retrieve presents for her. She opened the box. There were jewels of all kinds, rubies, emeralds and diamonds. She retrieved a small black pouch and emptied its contents into her hand. Out fell over a hundred diamonds large and small. She put them back into the pouch and stuffed it into her bra. She put the box back in its place. She sat down in a chair and waited for about two hours. It was the normal time for the Prince to be done with her and to have fallen asleep. The wait was good for her. Her body stopped trembling and her mind regained its focus. When the time was up, she went back to the bathroom and strapped the knife back onto her thigh. She put her dress back on, which was still wet, but because it was black it did not show that much. She let herself out and walked up to one of the guards outside.

"Bring me to Mr. Za.; I have an urgent message from His Highness for him." Her tone was firm and authoritative. Without hesitating, the guard led the way towards Mr. Za's quarters walking at a brisk pace. When they reached Mr. Za's quarters, she turned to the guard and said, "You may go now." He left without having looked at her or saying a word. She knocked loudly on Mr. Za's door, but there was no sound coming from the room, so she knocked again, louder this time. She heard some shuffling from inside the room and Mr. Za opened the door; he had obviously been asleep.

"What is it, what do you want?"

"I must speak to you, Mr. Za, it is urgent, the Prince has sent me. May I come in please?" Without waiting for his reply, she took a step forward and he let her pass.

"Yes, yes, come in." He closed the door behind her.

She turned to face him. "I must go to the bathroom first, Mr. Za. I'll only be a minute."

"Yes of course, it's over there." He pointed to an open door across the room. Aisha went quickly towards the door as if she had a pressing need to go to the bathroom. Inside, she retrieved the knife and flushed the toilet. She took a deep breath and opened the door. Mr. Za was sitting on a sofa, rubbing his eyes. She walked over to him, one hand behind her back, holding the knife. He looked up at her.

"Well girl, what is this message from His Highness? Speak up now, it's the middle of the night, you know."

"The Prince told me to tell you," she paused, "that you're an ignorant pig whose mother was a whore and that the reason you smell so bad is that as any pig, you spend too much time in your own shit." Aisha spoke calmly in Arabic, looking him straight in the eyes. Mr. Za bolted to his feet, standing only a few feet from her.

"What!" he shouted. "What did you say? The Prince never told you this, no, these are your words, you lowlife whore. I will teach you to come in here in the middle of the night and to say such things about my mother." He took two steps forward, hand upraised. Before he could land his blow, Aisha plunged the knife into his chest, both hands on the handle; she put all the power of her body into the blow. She struck him in the region of the heart. His eyes bulged out of proportion from the surprise. He let out an "Ah, ah, ah…" and clutched the knife with both hands; their eyes were locked into each other's.

"What, what is this?" he managed to utter.

Aisha ripped the knife out of his chest for a response, cutting his hands in the process. She struck him three more times violently and he fell backwards on the sofa. She stood over him triumphantly. Mr. Za just looked at her, dazed, in shock, life quickly draining out of him.

"Now Mohamed, let's see if we can take care of your loneliness, what do you say?" She got on her knees and lifted his robe, grabbing his penis with one hand. He lifted a hand feebly to protest, unable to move or make a sound. With a swift movement of the razor-sharp knife, she cut off his penis. He swooned, eyes turning in his head. She grabbed him by the nose, opening his mouth and stuffed the severed penis into his mouth. As he gasped for air with the bloody organ sticking out of his mouth, she struck him again and again with the knife, until she had no more strength left in her arms and had to stop. She stared at him for a while, content with her deed and happy that he was dead and could therefore harm her no more. Her heart was pounding madly. Once she got her breath back, she rose, went to the bathroom, and cleaned herself up. She stepped back into the room, put all the lights out and waited for about thirty minutes. Then, she let herself out and walked briskly over to Mr. Chen's door.

She knocked on the door, looking around nervously. There was no answer or noise coming from the room. She knocked again, a bit louder and more insistent this time, still no answer. She knocked even louder and then she heard a noise coming from the room. The door opened, and Mr. Chen looked at her squinting.

"What's going on? What do you want? Do you know what time it is?" He did not notice the hand behind her back nor the dark spot on the front of her dress.

"I must speak to you, Mr. Chen, it is most urgent. I come at the request of the Prince. May I come in?"

He opened the door to let her in. "Very well, girl, come in. I do hope this is important." She walked in and quickly turned to face him so that he did not get to see the knife in the movement.

He stood there still holding the half-open door.

"Well, what?" He looked at her, perplexed.

"Please shut the door, Mr. Chen. I shall not be long, I promise, and the Prince has asked that I be discreet." He shut the door and faced her. "Before I tell you the Prince's message Mr. Chen, I need to know if you ever did to my mother, what you did to me the other day."

He looked at her in disbelief, "what, you wake me in the middle of the night for this? The Prince wants to know this? Are you kidding me or what? If you had told the Prince about the lesson I gave you, I would be dead already. You may be a whore, but you're not a stupid whore. You want your family to live, so you have kept silent and now you're making me very angry with these questions in the middle of the night. I think you're due for another lesson girl." He took a step forward and Aisha stepped back, but he continued to move in her direction.

"You know what else, you stupid cow? Your mother is a whore, just like you and just like you; I have had to teach her a few lessons about who is in charge. Does that satisfy you, you ignorant little slut?" He was shouting now and very angry. "Now come over here and let me show you again what is good for you and your mother, you bitch." He stretched out his arms in a gesture to grab her, but Aisha pounced forward to meet his thrust; she was holding the knife with both hands and she plunged it into his chest to the very handle.

"This is from her and me, you pervert!" she shouted. She removed the blade from his chest and he fell to his knees, looking at her in utter disbelief.

"Oh, oh, oh, you stupid, stupid girl, you will pay for this, oh you will pay for this." He vacillated slightly. Aisha went behind him and kicked him in the back. He fell facedown on the carpet, blood oozing out of him. She grabbed him by the hair and lifted his head.

"Die, you piece of shit." With a swift movement, she slit his throat open then let his head drop. She then proceeded to cut open his silk pajamas and ripped them off. With a powerful stroke, she planted the knife up his anus and left it there.

"Burn in hell, you pig!" she yelled at the dying Chen. She stood over him defiant and spit at him. For the third time that night, she washed up and then headed silently back to the House of the Pure.

Once inside her room, Aisha was violently ill. She cried and couldn't stop trembling for over an hour. Once she regained her composure, she cleaned herself, changed her clothes, and went to fetch Mohini.

"Come quickly to my room, be silent and bring tea," Aisha whispered to the half-awake Mohini. Twenty minutes later, she arrived in Aisha's room with a tea tray.

"What is going on? It is the middle of the night; you seem so agitated, what's wrong? Did he beat you again?" Mohini was worried; she did not like the feeling of the moment.

Aisha did not answer right away and she took one of her hands in hers. "Mohini, my beloved Mohini, now is not the time for questions. You know you are like a second mother to me and I need you now to make me a promise, a promise that you will never break, ever, no matter what happens. Can you do that?" Aisha's gaze was intense and solemn.

"Yes, but what is it, child? What has happened that you should wake me in the middle of the night and ask me to make a promise to you?"

"Say I promise that what I say here will forever be our secret. Say it, Mohini."

She took one of Aisha's hands. "I promise, ok, now tell me what this is all about."

Aisha retrieved the pouch filled with diamonds from her bra and put it in Mohini's hand. "I want you to take this to my mother when you leave next month for your holidays. You may sell a stone or two to pay for you and your husband's trip. The rest is for her. You know I trust you more that anything. You must do this for me, Mohini."

"But what stones are you talking about, child?"

Aisha opened the pouch and dumped the contents into one of her hands. Mohini looked at the diamonds and then to Aisha.

"Where did you get these? Have you stolen them? My God, girl, you frighten me. This is insanity, if they come from where I think they come from."

"No questions, please, just promise you will do as I ask, please Mohini." Aisha looked at her, her eyes filled with love and trust.

"Ok, I will do as you wish, but tell me what happened and where did you get these?"

"Hush now, no questions. Do you trust me, Mohini?"

"Yes, of course I trust you, you know that. I love you as much as I love my own daughters."

"Fine then, leave it at that, speak of this to no one, no one, do you understand? Your own life depends on your silence, ok?"

"Yes, I understand, oh, but I'm so worried about you." Mohini's eyes filled with tears. Aisha took her in her arms and stroked her hair.

"Don't be, my Mohini, don't be. All will be well, I promise you, ok?"

"Ok then." They held onto each other for a long time.

After many reassurances, tears and promises, Mohini finally went back to her room with the diamond-filled pouch.

Aisha did not sleep that night. She sat in a chair on her balcony and watched the sun rise.

They came for her early the next morning. Four guards entered her room. Without a word, they grabbed her and took her away. They brought her to a building she had never seen before. It was a small prison; in the basement were cells. They beat her severely before locking her up. The cell was dark, humid, and most inhospitable. She had a large cut over her eye that had bled down her face. Her lower lip was swollen and her whole left side ached badly. She lay on the floor in the dark for a long time. With great difficulty, she got up and sat on the mattress-less metal cot. There was a pail half filled with water in a corner. High above her, about twenty feet or so, was a very small barred opening, from which the only light came in. She sat there for hours, hurting badly, thinking of her mother and sisters. Tears rolled down her face, mixing with the blood and soiling her robe. All day she just lay there, in pain and in shock, falling in and out of sleep.

She was awakened the next day by the noise of the cell door being unlocked. The cell was dark and the light that poured in from the open door hurt her eyes. A guard looked in. He deposited a piece of bread and a tin cup on the floor and closed the door. Aisha shuffled over and picked up the bread and began to eat it slowly. Her mouth hurt a lot, but she was starving, so it felt good. In the tin cup was water, which she did not all drink, saving some for later. When she was done, she shuffled back to the cot and lay down. She was cold and suffered from her bruises, but she was serine and calm, she knew what was coming and was ready.

On the afternoon of the third day, the cell door opened and Mr. Rowling stepped into the cell. The guard left the door open and stood at attention outside. Aisha was sitting on the cot; he walked over to where she was and stood over her.

"Aisha, my poor child, what in God's name have you done? I had to pull a lot of strings to get in here to see you. Look at you, my God, what have they done to you?" He sat down on the cot beside her.

"I did what I had to do, Mr. Rowling. I could not take their abuse any longer; it was all just too much."

"Tell me what happened. We have very little information. All I have been able to find out is that the Prince and Mr. Za are dead, and by your hand, they say. Is this true?"

"Yes, it is true, Mr. Rowling, they got what they deserved. I regret nothing."

"But that is terrible, Aisha. Do you understand what this means? These people do not deal in a gentle manner with someone who has done such a thing."

"I know what will happen, Mr. Rowling and I am prepared for my fate." She stared at the dirt floor, a determined look on her face.

"I read your manuscript this morning, Aisha. I'm sorry I did not keep my promise to you, but when I heard what had happened and that you were the one responsible; I just had to read it. I understand you now. I am so sorry." The reserved Rowling put a hand on hers in a gesture of sympathy.

"You must get that manuscript out to the world, Mr. Rowling. It must be known what kind of an animal the Prince was and what goes on here."

"Can you tell me what happened the other night? I think it is important that this information be added to your manuscript." He pulled out a small notebook and a pen from his jacket pocket. "Do you feel up to it?"

"Yes I do, Mr. Rowling, I am ready." So Aisha told him the whole story of the fatal evening when she had killed the Prince, Mr. Za, and Mr. Chen. She left out no sordid details. Had the cell not been so dark, she would have noticed Mr. Rowling's face turn red a few times. When she was done, he put the notebook hastily back in his pocket.

"Wow," he said, "I must say I would never have thought you capable of such acts. It is most disconcerting, but then again, these people, these men, were horribly inappropriate towards you and I guess in a way, they had it coming." They were both silent for a moment.

"Now this is what I will do, Aisha. I will get this story out, I promise you. I don't know how yet, but I swear I will. You will not have done..." He stopped mid-sentence suddenly embarrassed about what he was about to say.

Aisha reassured him, "Its ok, Mr. Rowling, do not worry about me, I will be fine. I have said my prayers and am at peace with my God and myself. Just get my story out, please. Now may I ask you one last small favor, sir?"

"Tell me, what is it?"

"I wish that you would write to my mother and tell her what has happened to me and that I love her and my sisters very much." She put her face in her hands and began to weep silently. Rowling put his hand on her shoulders.

"I will, Aisha, just give me the address and I promise I will." Aisha gave him the indications he needed to contact her mother and sisters.

"I must be going now. I have been here too long already. I wish you all the courage you will need, Aisha Sayuno, and I am glad that life has put you on my path. I will not let you down, I promise."

"Thank you, sir; you are one of the kindest persons I have ever met. I shall never forget you." She kissed his hands. Rowling got up and left the cell. The guard closed the door behind him. Aisha stayed sitting on her cot, motionless and calm, as calm as she had ever been. The visit of Mr. Rowling had been a godsend.

On the fifth day of her incarceration, four guards entered her cell in the morning. They grabbed her and tied her hands behind her back. They led her away. She was put in the back of a military truck and driven towards the city. She was taken in front of a tribunal of sorts. Three men sat at a long table. All wore traditional robes, with long gray beards and severe looks on their faces. The guards pushed her in front of them. There was no one else in the hall. One of them began to read from a document in Arabic. It was a description of her crimes. Most of the gory details had been omitted. Once the accusations had been read, the man in the middle spoke.

"Do you recognize these crimes as your own?" he asked in Arabic.

"Yes I do," she answered firmly in Arabic.

The man in the middle looked from side to side to the two other men and they nodded their heads.

"You have confessed to these crimes in front of this court and therefore, according to the laws of this country, you are sentenced to be beheaded publicly. The sentence shall be carried out before sundown on Friday. Do you have anything else to say?"

"No, I do not," she answered.

"Then may the almighty have mercy on you, this court is adjourned." They rose and filed out. The guards took Aisha by the arms and led her away. It had all lasted thirty minutes at the most. It was all a blur to Aisha, and anyway, she was past the point of caring.

When she was back in her cell, she realized that Friday was the next day, one more day to live. She prayed all night and visions of her mother and sisters filled her mind. "I love you all so much," she said out loud as she looked up to the small opening that let in the light of the moon.

"Forgive me, Mama, forgive me, it was more than I could bear." She cried softly and rocked herself gently on the edge of the cot.

They came for her the next day late in the afternoon. Her hands were still tied behind her back from the day before. The guards checked if the ropes were still tight around her wrists. They took her away, pushing her and kicking her along. She remained of stone. Nothing they could do could be worse that what she had been through.

They arrived at a public square. There was a large crowd massed around a high wooden platform. The army truck drove right up to the platform. The guards took her out and walked her up the steps. In the middle of the platform was a large solid wooden block not more than two feet high. A man stood beside it, a large strong man. In his hands he held a large saber whose blade was short and thick. He did not look at her; he was gazing steadily into the crowd. All were silent, all eyes on her. For a moment, nothing seemed to move; the air was of an eerie stillness. The guards brought her in front of the wooden block. A guard held onto each one of her arms and two others stood close behind her. All stood there in silence for a moment, probably waiting for a signal of some sorts to proceed. Aisha decided to seize the moment and with all the rage within her and all the power of her lungs she yelled out in Arabic,

"The pigs are dead, the pigs are dead, the pigs are dead."

Her shouts caught everyone by surprise. For a split second, no one moved, and then quickly, the guards holding her arms grabbed her and pushed her down on her knees, body onto the block; the two guards behind her held her legs down. The suddenness of the movement knocked the wind out of her and at that instant she saw her mother's face, smiling to her,

"Go now, go my child," she said, in her soft, singing voice. "Go join your father, he is waiting for you. He loves you, I love you; we all love you."

With a rapid swish, the savage saber sliced the air and Aisha's head rolled onto the platform with a thud. The crowd roared; this is what they had come for and so ended the life of Aisha Sayuno.

***

Six weeks after the day Aisha was executed, Christopher Rowling and Daniel Madden met for drinks at Rowling' posh private club in London, three weeks had passed since their chance encounter at the Paris airport. Madden had sent Christopher his draft of Aisha's story and the four-part series derived from it that his newspaper would soon print.

"Hello there, Christopher, how have you been?"

"Fine, thank you Madden, please, won't you sit down. Would you like a drink?"

"Thank you Christopher, I'll have the usual." Rowling motioned to an elderly waiter to come over, and he ordered a drink for Madden.

"So, Madden, you have been very busy I see. I read with great interest the story you wrote and the four articles you derived from it. I must admit, it is rather well written and I do appreciate the fact that you have admirably kept my name out of the articles. Although in the story, you have done no such thing, but then again, the story is not for publication, of course."

"Thank you, Christopher. We will be running the first article in the Saturday edition of the paper. The series will be called 'Aisha, Sex Slave to the Royal Family.' It is powerful material and will most certainly make some major waves." Madden purposely did not answer the other's query. "So Christopher, may I call you Sir Rowling now?"

Rowling laughed, remembering their little episode in Paris about his being knighted. "You may now, Madden. It is perfectly appropriate and exact." He laughed again and raised his glass in Daniel's direction.

"So look, Christopher, to get back to the story of Aisha, I have something I want to ask you."

Rowling looked up from his drink to the American. "Yes, and what may that be?"

"Well seeing that you are now knighted and all, don't you think that if your name did come out in connection with this story, don't you think that you are untouchable now? I mean, they are not going to take your title away, right? As for the royal family, well, they will get what they deserve for having let the Prince do as he wished for so long. I mean, come on, Christopher, they knew what was going on. They knew he was buying girls in Third World countries under false pretexts and then made them literally sex slaves in his palace. There is no way that they did not know. Are they not guilty by association? They stood by while this guy was beating, raping, and killing young women every day. Now you cannot be insensitive to all this, Christopher? I think the whole story has to come out. I want to publish it in book form, as a follow-up to the four articles."

Rowling looked at Daniel for a long time before saying, "I was there when they beheaded her, you know."

"I know, you told me all about it in Paris, remember, in the hotel lobby."

"It was one of the worst days of my life, Madden. I was sitting with these people, these people who permitted this situation to deteriorate to the point that it did, these people who watched, as this beautiful, innocent, abused girl was beheaded, like an animal brought to slaughter, while the crowd jeered on. It was the worst day of my life, Madden, I swear." Rowling stared blankly ahead, lost in his thoughts.

"Does that mean yes, Christopher? Are you saying that you give me your permission to do this? There will be waves for you if I do; you know that, don't you?"

Rowling came out of his reverie and looked Daniel straight in the eyes. "You know what, Madden? I don't give a damn, to hell with them all. As for my title, well, if Her Majesty thinks that I should be stripped of it for having told the truth, well, to hell with her too."

"Wow, those are pretty strong words for a Brit there, Christopher. Well ok, but what about the Prince's family? They might seek revenge, you know. They are vicious people when it comes to their reputation."

"I am an old man, Madden, let them come after me. At least I will have died an honorable man. No, go for it I say, do it man, I'm with you." He raised his glass.

"Allow me to propose a toast, Madden." Their glasses touched. "To Aisha, may her sufferings have not been in vain."

"Yes Christopher, to Aisha."

***

At about the same time, halfway across the planet, another kind of reunion was going on. Mohini, after having given herself much trouble, had found Aisha's mother. With the help of her husband, she had brokered some diamonds. Of course they had been grossly underpaid, but still it was a lot of money for these humble people. The money had permitted them to buy plane tickets and to seek Lina Sayuno out. They had found her and her daughters exactly where Aisha had left them four years before. It was an emotional and heartbreaking encounter. Mohini told her the whole story of what happened to her daughter, omitting some particularly horrible details. Finally, Lina Sayuno knew what had happened to her daughter, of whom she had had no news for over a year. She had tried everything possible with her limited means in that period of time, but Mr. Chen had been nowhere to be found and desperation had settled in. Mohini, who arrived before Rowling's letter, did not bring the news she had hoped for, but at least now she knew. Lina and

Mohini cried and hugged and held hands in her humble dwelling.

"I miss her so much, Mohini, she was the beacon of my darkness, I miss her so," tears rolled down her cheeks.

Mohini kissed her hands, "me too, Lina, me too, I miss her so."

THE END

ABOUT THE AUTHOR

Ian Tremblay works in the entertainment business and is an avid world traveller and fishing aficionado. He studied English Literature and has self-published three other books, *Tales of Inhumanity and Retribution, Tales of Duplicity and Discontent* and *The Illegal and the Refugee-An American Love Story.*

THE ILLEGAL AND THE REFUGEE - An American Love Story is a tale of tragedy and triumph that highlights the difficulties and the hardships of Latino immigration to the United States. With roots set deep in Mexico and Cuba, it is a story about letting go of the past, the resilience of the human spirit in the face of adversity and of deep, unconditional love.

If you wish to find out more about the author go to his website **www.iantremblay.com**